Looking Back

The Final Tale of Life on the Prairie

Looking Back

The Final Tale of Life on the Prairie

Linda K. Hubalek

Butterfield Books, Inc.
Lindsborg, Kansas

Looking Back: The Final Tale of Life on the Prairie
© 1994 by Linda K. Hubalek
Fourth Printing 1999
Printed in the United States of America

For information about Hubalek's books, see the list at the back of this book, or write to **Butterfield Books, Inc.**, PO Box 407, Lindsborg, KS 67456-0407. phone: 785-227-2707, fax: 785-227-2017, website: www.bookkansas.com

Photos courtesy of Rozella Schaeffer, except for the following:
   Assaria Lutheran Church, Pages xii, xiii, xiv, 40.
   Verna Berry, Page 18.
   Linda Hubalek, Pages 72, 73, 74, 79.
   Lester and Ione Johnson, Pages v, 47.
   Maurine Johnson, Page 38.
   Lowell Miller, Page 36.
   Carl Peterson, Page 41.
   Laurina Redden, Page 39.
   Smoky Valley Genealogical Society, Pages 116-119.

Publisher's Cataloging in Publication
   (Prepared by Quality Books Inc.)

Hubalek, Linda K.
Looking back : the final tale of life on the prairie
Linda K. Hubalek. --1st ed.
p. cm. -- (Butter in the well series ; 4)
Includes bibliographical references.
Preassigned LCCN: 94-74378
ISBN 1-886652-03-1
1. Runeberg, Kajsa--Fiction. 2. Swedish Americans--Kansas--Saline County--Fiction. 3. Farm life--Kansas--Saline County--Fiction. 4. Saline County (Kan.)--Fiction. 5. Historical fiction. 6. Diary fiction. I. Title. II. Series.
PS3558.U19L66 1994   913'.54
                                QB194-1741

To my parents, Lester and Ione Johnson, who have lived on this farm for 48 years.

Books by Linda K. Hubalek

Butter in the Well
Prärieblomman
Egg Gravy
Looking Back
Trail of Thread
Thimble of Soil
Stitch of Courage
Planting Dreams
Cultivating Hope
Harvesting Faith

Acknowledgments

I would like to express my sincerest thanks to all of the people who helped with *Looking Back*. The memories recalled by dear friends, family and neighbors who have lived in Liberty Township, have given this book the authenticity it needed to tell the real-life happenings of the people and the area. I hope you like how I portrayed your community.

A last special thank you to Julia, for writing down your mother's stories; to Mabel, for snapping pictures of your family and farm, and to Rozella, for sharing both with me.

Tack så mycket.

Linda Katherine Johnson Hubalek

Table of Contents

Peter and Kajsa, with their daughters, Julia and Mabel

Foreword

The Butter in the Well series is based on the life of Maja Kajsa Svensson Runeberg, who homesteaded my family's farm in Saline County, Kansas, in 1868. In the first book, *Butter in the Well*, people realize Kajsa was a real person facing the challenges and dangers of homesteading on the wild prairie. She came alive and flourished—almost as a heroine; a Swedish immigrant that met the struggles of the land, nurtured a family, established a farm and started a community.

The story of the family continues through *Prärieblomman: The Prairie Blossoms for an Immigrant's Daughter,* using Alma Eleanor Swenson, the third child of the family, as the main character. Even though the reader isn't reading Kajsa's direct thoughts, they see how she matures and changes along with her children, as they become adults and start their own families.

Egg Gravy, the third book, is an interlude, a build up before the climax of the final tale of Kajsa. By pulling out quotes from the first two books and featuring recipes gleaned from the original homesteader's cookbooks and files, it helps the reader of the series understand the everyday domestic life of the pioneer woman.

Looking Back finishes my version of the personal first-person account of Kajsa Runeberg. I have woven known facts—dates, pictures, family stories—then added personal feelings that must go through a person's mind as they sort through their belongings to move from the place they have lived for 51 years.

I based this book mainly on three documents I found: the purchase of the house in Salina that Peter and Kajsa moved into; the Swedish minutes of the Hallville *Kvinnornas Missionsförening* (Women's Missionary Society), stating Kajsa hosted the group at her home for the July 20th meeting; and the public notice in the Salina newspaper announcing the Runeberg farm sale on July 24th.

Some of Kajsa's belongings that are still in the possession of myself or family members, were worked into the story. Photos taken by Mabel and neighbors gave graphic descriptions of the farm and community like it was in that time period. Memories of the people who lived or visited the house and farm since Kajsa left, helped mold the scenes.

In June, I walked the farm Kajsa homesteaded and drove around Liberty township, retracing the steps Kajsa would have taken before she left the farm. During the last two weeks in July, I wrote most of this book—an eerie feeling, being 75 years to the week that these events in Kajsa's life happened.

Kajsa was one of the multitude of immigrants that had to leave the life and land they knew and start over in another country. She must have had an ocean of emotions as she looked back on her childhood life in Sweden and her adult life on the land she staked in 1868. I wove my own feelings of leaving this farm with the sentiment Kajsa must have had at closing this chapter in her life.

We have all had to leave a place we loved at one point in time.

Mabel and Julia

Hallville Kvinnornas Missionsförening

Members

Mrs. Rev. Ericson
Mrs. Nels Johnson
Mrs. Chas. Peterson
Mrs. P. Almquist
Mrs. Elof Peterson
Mrs. J. O. Linn
Mrs. Peter Runneberg
Mrs. B. Mattson
Mrs. Joe Olson
Mrs. Martin Johnson
Mrs. Andrew Swenson
Mrs. J. S. Olson
Mrs. Peter Isaacson
Mrs. Anton Bloomberg
Mrs. Andrew Johnson
Mrs. Ella Carlson
Mrs. Anna Stenfors
Mrs. Arthur Johnson

List of Members- 1919

Prologue

July 20, 1919

The Setting

A slightly stooped woman with white hair in a bun, stands in the parlor doorway, making sure everything is ready for the women that will meet in her house this afternoon.

Everything is in place. All is quiet except for the ticking of the mantel clock.

A tear slowly wanders down her lined face as she looks back into the room once more.

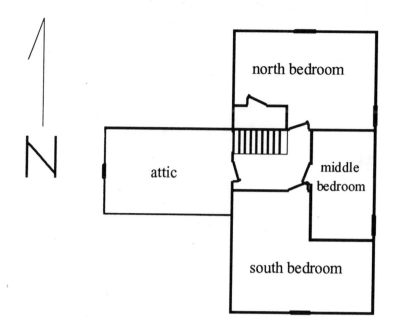

Upper floor of Kajsa's house

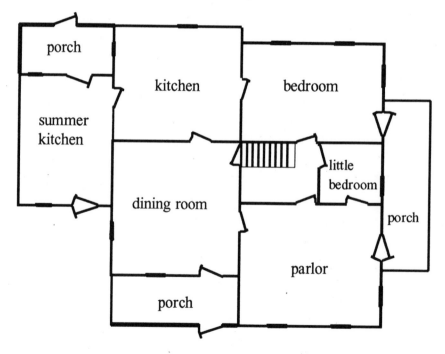

Main floor of Kajsa's house

Sunday, July 20th

With one foot on the threshold, I pause in the doorway, hesitating to leave the parlor. As if drawn by a magnet, I turn back to face the room I was about to leave.

I survey the scene, mentally making sure everything is in order. Our fancy parlor chairs and plain dining room ones line the room in a circle, ready for company. The massive rocker is reserved for the speaker and is placed so the afternoon sun won't blind him through the south window.

Besides the wooden rocking chair, two rose-colored upholstered chairs, a matching love seat and a glider rocker grace the room. The small, dark wood parlor table with curved legs sits between the windows on the south wall. Covered with a large white crocheted doily, it holds the red glass kerosene lamp that lights the room in the evenings.

The upright piano in the southwest corner has the proper hymnal on its music rack for Julia to use for accompanying our group when we sing our hymn during the meeting. Various sheet music and books from several eras and tastes have graced the rack over time as the children and their friends used the piano for their entertainment. The dark green, gold-rimmed bowl, received as a present, is centered on top of the piano, while two of the conch shells Willie brought from California rest on both ends. Cream and gray cardboard frames with family studio photos are scattered among these items.

Ornate gold frames encasing three painted-on-glass landscape pictures adorn the main spaces on the walls. The mother-of-pearl

1

West wall of parlor

on the glass makes the moon shimmer on my favorite picture of a castle beside a stone bridge. The other two are ocean scenes with the water glistening in the light. Family pictures fill smaller spaces. Diamond-shaped ruby glass frames of Julia and Mabel are on the west wall. Embroidered and needlepoint pillows and my sansevieria plant have found conspicuous places on the floor around the furniture.

The multi-floral area rug is clean of lint and farmyard gatherings. The furniture and dark wood baseboards gleam from their last-minute polishing. By evening though, a new film of dust from the dirt road just outside the room will change it back to its usual state. The outside parlor door is open, ready to invite my friends in. Three flies make a continuous search on the green painted, wood-trimmed screen door, trying to find a way into the house.

As I put my hand on the door frame, ready to leave the room a second time, I stare at each item again, as if looking for the first time, wondering about its' existence, the reason it is in this room.

When did we get that rocker? It's been a fixture in our house for years. *How many children did I rock to sleep in it? Did we get it before Julia, or Mabel was born?*

How many years has that picture been hanging on the south wall? It doesn't seem to be as brilliant as I remember. *When did it start to fade?*

Which sister crocheted the table doily? I can't believe my memory has faded on such important mementos from a family member.

I do remember buying the parlor lamp. Many lamps have graced this room as it was transformed from a bedroom to the parlor over the years. It is hard to imagine that fifty years ago we were burning duck feathers in tallow to dimly light our cramped dugout.

The parlor is eerily quiet, except for the rhythmic tick-tock of the clock. The sun casts shadowed moving shapes across the area rug as the breeze moves the heavy white lace curtains that dip across the room's three windows. The heavy victorian brocade wallpaper gives the room a sense of elegance, but I can see through the paper and remember building this simple wood-framed addition onto our original one-room stone house.

Echoes of yesterday slowly erase the present and draw me into the past.

Pound! Pound! Pound!
Sometimes our hammers are in unison as Carl and I pound the square-head nails into the lumber. Other times it is an off-beat echo. I push another strand of damp hair out of my eyes, as I taste my salty sweat that drips onto my lip. My rough calloused hand automatically reaches into my apron pocket for another nail. We're both balancing on ladders, leaned high against the new two-story addition to our house. Nine-year-old Christina and six-year-old Willie hand up another piece of siding, while little Alfred and Alma play in the shade of the house. Carl positions his end of the long piece of siding, and looks to me to do the same before we lift our hammers and pound again. We need each other to keep the other end balanced; not only with the siding, but also in life.

It is finally soaking into my brain. This is the last day this room—this house—looks normal, lived in, everything clean and in its place.

Tomorrow we start the process of packing our possessions, to leave the house I've lived in for 49 years. Where have the years gone?

Turning back and stepping across the threshold into the dining room, I see in my mind's eye the rough sandstone walls of our first home, which is this dining room.

Oh, how I loved this first house. After two years of living underground in the dugout and scraping our meager income together from the toil and sweat of breaking the sod and raising a crop, it was sheer delight to be living above ground. My prayers had been answered. Life was finally getting easier and we were making progress. Most of the material for building the walls still came from the rock outcroppings in the area, but we bought windows, and lumber and shingles for the roof. Family and neighbors helped whenever they could, but Carl and I did most of the work. This single room was our whole house for several years, until we could afford to build more rooms. Our whole family and everything we owned, fit into this 16 by 16 foot space.

I was so excited to finally have braided rag rugs on the plank floor instead of buffalo hides that covered the dugout's earthen floor. It seemed almost strange to have a dry surface instead of the muddy floor we'd have during a rain or a wet season where the water table would seep up through the ground. Snakes, toads and earthworms didn't have to be swept out daily from the corners or under the bed.

Red gingham curtains framing real windows delighted me for years and still put a smile on my face. I was so proud when I finally had the money to buy that material.

A crude hand-hewn table with side benches crowded the south end of the room. It was the center of attention. Besides being used to serve us meals, it was the work space for everything from making bread to repairing harnesses. The only glass lantern we owned, revered, and took great care of, shined in the middle of the table so the children could study their school and church lessons at night after they did their chores. Many important discussions and decisions in our lives were made while sitting at that table.

Our mainstay on the west wall, the wood stove fueled by cow chips and corn cobs, kept us and the occasional company warm.

Whether it was dirt-poor immigrants like ourselves passing through on a cold fall night, or leery Indians needing to get out of a winter blizzard, all were welcome because it was the law of the land. Besides, we were alone on the desolate prairie and we hungered to talk to someone that had news from the outside world.

Meals first fixed over a campfire, and later this stove, varied with the time of year and what was available. Our first food was only what we could find on the land. There was no grocery store within 16 miles; besides we had no money to purchase such supplies. Small game, like rabbits, quail and possums were bountiful, as were catfish, turtles and frogs from the river. Carl tried to trap or snare food to save bullets. Deer and buffalo were only hunted during fall and winter when the meat could be preserved in the cold weather. We survived, but we hungered for fruits and vegetables which were non-existent except for a few plums and wild grapes during a brief time in the summer. Milk and coffee was beyond our means without money to purchase a cow or coffee beans.

As we broke the sod and planted the field crops and gardens, the next barrier was money to buy crocks and jars to store the produce in. The first few years everything had to be eaten fresh, dried and stored in simple cloth sacks (that occasionally were also filled with beetles eating our food), or buried in a grass-lined pit in the ground below the frost line.

As we were able to harvest our crops and have grain to trade, we accumulated various containers until we had hundreds in the cellar. We were still dependent on the land to provide us with something to fill the jars though. Some falls the cellar was brimming with a bountiful summer's harvest. Other years, like 1874, when the grasshopper and drought hit Kansas and wiped out our entire farm, I scrounged to make do with what little we had.

There was no luxury of a private bedroom area in this first room. Our simple wooden-frame bed with a feather ticking mattress protruded out of the east wall. The children slept on a trundle bed that was pulled out at night and pushed underneath our bed during the day. For naps during the day, they slept in our bed so we didn't trip over their bed.

Bedding consisted of a variety of animal hides we had tanned from animals we used for food, and quilts made from every scrap of material I could save. The luxury of white sheets was not even considered a remote possibility during our first years.

Simple shelves and pegs held all the limited clothing and bedding we owned. A dress or two for everyday use, be it working inside the house or outside behind the plow, was all I owned except for one good dress I religiously saved for church and special occasions. Our clothes were worn almost past the thread-bare stage before we would dip into our meager savings to buy material for new clothing. Even then I used what I could salvage from the folds of my dress skirt to fashion the children's clothing. Socks and winter garments were knitted, not bought. We went barefoot during the summer to save our shoe leather for winter.

Crude steps resembling a ladder led up the wall to the unfinished loft which was our only extra space for dry storage. A small window on the west end provided a little light. The trunk we brought from Sweden, and a few other boxes of items straddled the ceiling joists. We didn't go to the extra expense of flooring the room except for a narrow strip from the ladder to the window at the opposite end. Since it wasn't insulated, it was very hot during the summer and very cold during the winter. Occasionally we did have a guest who would sleep upstairs, but it certainly wasn't comfortable sleeping.

Right now, I'd almost like to reverse the clock and go back to that little space in our one-room house when our children were young.

Now the stone walls are plastered and papered, concealing their humble beginnings. Stylish curtains replaced the homespun gingham ones. A smaller heating stove doesn't take up as much space as the big cook stove that was moved to the kitchen. The old table is now stored in the granary and used for outdoor jobs like butchering.

I survey a different table today, covered with a snowy white linen cloth and laden with refreshments for this afternoon's meeting.

In the center of the table is a simple, perfect looking iced cake on a glass stand. As a rough estimate, I've cracked thousands of eggs for this eleven-egg angel food recipe. When I first started cooking, I had many failures until I learned to start with a cool oven when baking an angel food cake. Through years of practice, it is now almost automatic and they come out of the oven without a crack or burnt sides.

Warmed by the afternoon sunbeams streaming onto the table from the west window, the mellow aroma of fresh peach slices swimming in the clear glass bowl of sugar syrup pricks my taste buds. The peaches were recently picked from our orchard and have been awaiting their fate in the cool cellar below this room.

A plate of delicate Swedish *smörbalekser* and butter-rich *spritz* round out the food selection on the serving table. I want nothing but the best for my guests today.

Plates, cups and silverware form bumps under the flour sack tea towels that cover them to keep the dust and flies off. With a twinge I remember wanting a set of dishes years ago, but we had no money to afford more than the bare necessities for our family, let alone extras like a set of china plates. But one year for Christmas I was surprised by the gift of a few plates, and the set was slowly built after that. Whenever we've had company, my good china plates have welcomed our guests with pride.

I walk past the table to the kitchen to listen to the boiling of the pot of egg coffee brewing on the stove. Even though it is a hot July afternoon, protocol calls for coffee. But a stoneware crock of iced lemonade sits in the shade of the back porch, ready to be brought in to quench the thirst of the children that will accompany their mothers.

A horse snorts as it is pulled to a stop beside our side gate. The clock chimes three o'clock as I glance outside the window and see neighbor Charlie Peterson help Alma, his wife, from their buggy. Pastor Erickson could not attend our meeting today, so Charlie is filling in like he does so often at our chapel. Another buggy stops and I see a grandchild spill out from under Julia's grasp to run across the farmyard in search of our barnyard kittens.

As the neighborhood women congregate and happily greet each other as they arrive, they don't realize the almost dark and foreboding feelings that are trying to crowd my mind. This is the last meeting I will host for the Hallville Women's Missionary Society.

Years ago I yearned for a female voice when I was alone on the prairie. My mission back then was to welcome every new woman into the community because I was lonely and I knew we would need to rely on each other. Now there are enough of us that we can help others in our community and our country.

Opening the parlor door wide for my friends, I give each one a hug as they pass over the threshold of the parlor door. Next month the group will meet without me. At the end of this week, I'll be leaving my lifelong circle of friends.

Like pieces of a puzzle, circumstances of life have made us realize that it is time to move from the farm, although I have fought the decision most of the way. At 75, it is harder to move around, keep up with the chores and yard work. Peter jokes in Swedish that "we will starve off the farm" but he would like to slow down, enjoy life and not have to spend sun up to sun down working the fields any longer. I wish one of our children would have considered moving to our home, but they all have had established farms of their own for years.

After much debating, we finally bought a house in Salina. Both Christine and Carrie live there, so we went that direction rather than Lindsborg. We signed the papers in May, but stayed on the farm until we harvested the summer wheat and oats.

The next, and last time our family and neighbors will join us at our home will be for our farm sale this Thursday. Farm equipment and tools accumulated over time will pass from our hands, through the auctioneer's to other farmers. Livestock, some knowing only our meadow and barn will be bewildered on another farm after they are auctioned. A couple of old favorite nurse cows will move next door to Joe and Julia's. Chickens will find themselves a new pen or a stew pot.

This whole week will be difficult, a whirlwind of emotions. As of yet, the full impact of what we are doing hasn't soaked in yet. I have mixed feelings of leaving the farm that I helped build. I want to leave with dignity and pride. I look forward to life in Salina, time to travel and visit our children and friends. Just imagine not having to get up with the chickens, milk the cow twice a day, and sweat in front of a hot stove to feed the threshing crews. Of course I'll still have household chores to do, but the new house shouldn't get as dirty being in town. It has the modern conveniences of indoor plumbing and electricity! No more trips to the outhouse during the day or emptying the chamber pot. Electrical light bulbs will illuminate the room with a turn of a switch instead of cleaning and refilling the kerosene lamps.

I still wonder if the modern conveniences in town are worth sacrificing my roots to this land.

As Charlie clears his throat, the chatter ceases around the circle of sixteen women that line the room's chairs. Everyone but me automatically bows their head for Charlie's opening prayer. I stare at the circle; feeling doomed that I haven't dropped by head, but I want to remember this picture of the women in my house.

Swedish prayers have played an important role in our lives, not only for simple things like blessing our meeting today, but comforting us when losing a partner or child. The older women of the group have lived through much suffering and trials as they toiled to homestead their land. We blazed the trail for our children. They will never have to worry about building a house from little of nothing, or taking care of a deathly ill child without the help of a doctor. We've built a community, and in the process assured our children a better life than if we had stayed in Sweden and never tackled the Kansas prairie.

Our circle has intertwined many times, encompassing several families as our children grew up and married another neighbor's child. Good friendships as classmates at Star and Wheeler Schools changed over the years to romantic intentions, and eventually marriage for many of our children the past twenty years. In many cases, like Magdalena's children and the Carlson and Peterson families, brother and sister married a sister and brother in a neighbor's family. That's how close this neighborhood is.

Our group is divided by age and experience. The older mothers, like Hannah Mattson and Anna Stenfors, who have each raised a large brood of children, surviving even after the deaths of children and husbands are still running their farms. The young ones, like Hulda Peterson and Emily Swenson, are just starting to raise a family. I wonder what will lay in store for these women in their next 50 years in the community.

My two sisters-in-law sit on either side of me, as if shielding me from the inevitable. I've always been beside them as my

9

brothers, their husbands, have left them alone on the farm, after their deaths. Magdalena eventually remarried and raised a second family. She and Nels recently moved off their farm to Lindsborg but she came back today to give me support.

Maria still lives on the farm that my younger brother, Andrew, homesteaded; but now their daughter, Millie, and her husband, Anton Bloomberg, have taken over the daily farm routine. As the older generation ages, it is good to know that the younger generation is staying in the community and taking care of the fields their parents broke as native sod years ago.

Is it too warm in here? I feel a trickle of sweat run down the front of my chest. My face is damp with perspiration beading on my forehead and upper lip. *Should I open another window, or will a gust of dirt layer a different kind of icing on the cake?* Worrying that this last meeting will not be perfect causes me a fluster of panic and I start to rise out of my chair. Daughter Julia senses my discomfort and passes her newest baby around the circle, nodding to the women in line that the baby needs to be in my lap immediately. Five-month-old Linette blinks and gives me a beautiful baby smile that melts my heart and comforts the passing concern. I'll miss not being next door to Julia's family, but I plan to have the time to visit all the children's children as soon as we get settled in the new house in town.

As Julia moves to the piano stool in preparation to accompany the singing, my mind flashes back to a little Julia, quietly entering the parlor and reaching on her tiptoes, shyly touching a single key on the pi-

Julia and Linette

ano to hear the sound her sisters make when they play the instrument. That was over 30 years ago. Now before I know it, Linnette will be doing the same thing.

Lillie Johnson reads the minutes of our last meeting and reports on our latest missionary project. Our Hallville group has helped many causes since we organized eight years ago in this very house. Before we built the Hallville Chapel, we were all members of the Assaria missionary group that started with the founding of the church in 1875. We've been fortunate to survive the prairie and build our farms and community, and we vowed to help others in dire need. We have raised money at concerts at Star School for the sufferers in Northern Sweden, sent trainloads of flour to the Cubans during the Spanish-American War, and supplies to the people who survived the San Francisco earthquake in 1906. Our latest major project that everyone was involved in was making and wrapping bandages for the soldiers of World War I. Everyone in the area worked for the cause. We knitted socks every spare minute, even during missionary meetings. Some of the women at this meeting had boys that went off to war; so it affected everyone in our tight neighborhood. Fortunately the war ended last November and the young men came home.

Unfortunately, besides the war, everyone here was also fighting the Spanish influenza. More soldiers died in camps from the flu than in the battles. We also lost close neighbors. The Rames family lost Esther and Olof within a week of each other.

The whole state was under quarantine. All public meetings, churches and schools were closed for several weeks last fall. The *Messiah* performances this spring were not performed until May because they had to delay the practices.

It was hard to help sick neighbors when the chance of your getting it and spreading it to your own family was a serious threat. Leaving cooked meals on their back porch and feeding their livestock was about all we could do for a sick family.

Neighbors helping neighbors. That's what this township and farming community is about. Neighbors automatically descended on our farm to get the corn picked when Carl died. Peter and I have traveled to all parts of the township to do the same when our neighbors were in need. I hope the next people who live on my farm will eventually sense the same feeling of belonging to this community.

The mingled laughter of the children grows closer as they come around the south corner of the house. They have checked out the barn, brooder house, old swing and who knows what else they shouldn't have gotten into, and are now ready for refreshments. Impatient that their mothers are still in the meeting, they have decided to check on the process of the meeting. As certain worried mothers follow the sound around to the front porch, they give a serious frown to the faces that just peaked into the screen door. The children back off as if stung by the glances and edge down to sit quietly on the edge of the porch floor. Knowing what was going on behind his back, Charlie knows its time to sum up his talk and dispense with the meeting.

Numb that my final meeting is almost over, I awkwardly stumble out of the parlor to the haven of my kitchen. Wiping my eyes with the corner of my apron, I compose myself, focusing on the mental list of items that must be brought into the dining room table to serve my guests. Automatically using the corner of my apron again, this time as hot pad, I lift the pot of coffee off the stove. I pour a half cup of coffee to check to make sure the coffee grounds and egg shells have settled to the bottom of the pot. Mabel brings in the lemonade while Julia uncovers the contents on the table.

It's tradition that the speaker and his wife are the first through the line for the refreshments, but he remarked that I should be the guest of honor and have the first cup since this is my last meeting. Fighting the lump growing in my throat, I told him I wanted the pleasure of serving my group this last time instead. Alma sensed my discomfort and lead Charlie through the line. The older women went through the line next, followed by the young mothers helping their impatient children.

My daughters tried to get me to sit back down with the group with my own plate and coffee, but I couldn't do it. Instead I kept asking if anyone wanted more coffee or cookies. Too soon they will all be gone.

Tack så mycket. Var så god. Even though my guests only said "thank you" as they left and I answered back "you're welcome" in our Swedish way, everyone knew it meant more. Thank you for being my neighbor ever since we tamed the prairie together, and thank you for being such a special friend all these years.

Supper consisted of leftovers from the ladies' coffee and a simple sandwich made from the noon's meat. Not feeling up to putting things away yet, I pushed the serving trays out of the way and we sat on the corner of the table to eat our meal. Peter wasn't very hungry since he sneaked into the kitchen several times today to snitch cookies. I don't feel like eating because of a churned up stomach. Mabel is even slightly subdued when she realizes this is the last Sunday supper meal we will eat together in this house.

Twilight is starting to darken the light coming through the parlor windows as I sink into a chair in the empty circle.

The wind, making a circle through the house, causes the parlor door to bump against the back of a chair that is holding it open. Visions of previous moments in this room flash through the back of my mind, like still pictures moving in rapid motion.

As I walk through the doorway, I spy Alma through the crack between the door and the frame, crouched down behind the parlor door, a hand over her mouth, trying to contain her giggling. It has been rainy, dreary weather for several days and the children are letting off steam by playing hide and seek this evening. I lean against the door, my full skirt hiding Alma as Willie flies past me, in hot pursuit of finding his hidden siblings.

My mind jumps forward, and the same little girl, now all grown up and wrapped in a cloud of white veil, is standing in the opposite corner of the parlor, intently staring at her groom as she quietly states her wedding vows.

Alma wondered if she would ever marry. Then Peter's brother, Nels, visited from Iowa and the sparks finally ignited over a year's worth of letter writing. Unfortunately that meant she moved to his farm and was no longer close by. Finally, after seven years, homesick Alma came home on the train for her first visit, with four little children, Arnold, Petunia, Lawrence and Florence, in tow. They

Alma's visit in 1918

arrived right after Thanksgiving and we hosted a huge celebration dinner in their honor. Besides the house being filled with family, neighbors overflowed the parlor when they stopped by all afternoon and evening to see Alma and her children. I think we baked more pies for that day than for a Star School social.

Being a typical parent, I wanted everything just right at home for her visit. There were a few things around the house that needed repair and remodeling, and I wanted it done before Alma arrived home. It didn't happen that way of course. The Palmquist Brothers of Lindsborg were contracted for the work and got the job done before Christmas. Alma spent this time visiting Willie and Minnie, and friends in Lindsborg to keep her children out of the worker's way.

When Peter opened the parlor door on Christmas Eve, the Christmas tree shone in the newly re-papered room. Of course the children dove toward the presents as their mothers felt and examined the walls. Our circle of children and grandchildren was complete, but we missed Nels, who stayed home to take care of the farm and animals. But there was one dull ache in at least mine and Marie, Alfred's wife's heart. They had lost a baby boy, Carl, earlier that year. I had lost a baby once too, so I know she was thinking that this child would never experience the joys of Christmas.

Never could I have comprehended that three grandchildren at this first Christmas together would not grow up to adulthood. Alma lost both Florence and Petunia to appendix ruptures, and Carrie lost Verna to pneumonia after measles complications.

Time went fast since Alma spent a week or so at each of her sibling's home, besides time here. In late January, Alma ushered her brood back on the train at Bridgeport and it was a long time before we saw them again.

She was here with Emmett and Alice, her youngest children last summer. Nels and the three older boys stayed home to take care of the summer crops.

Thinking of family, I have the urge to look through the photo album again. Striking a match against the side of the box, the flame dances as I lift the glass chimney and touch it to the awaiting wick. After adjusting the light so I could see clearly, I pull up a chair beside the table. Placing the back of the album on the edge of the table, directly underneath the light, I slowly open the

Alfred, Julia and Carrie

15

book and stare at the first picture.

The first picture in the album is the blurry photo of our homestead. Here we are lined up in front of the house, with the milk cows and the team of horses and buggy in the background to show how prosperous we were. A roaming photographer was in the area and I decided to splurge some egg money to have the photo taken. It must have been around 1881 or '82, before Peter and I married because he was standing on the side, instead of beside me.

Photographers and money were scarce during the early years. I don't have a picture of my first husband, Carl, or the older children as babies.

When Gröndal, the photographer moved into Lindsborg in 1887, I believe he was the busiest shop on Main Street. Families finally had a way to record their children and they took advantage of it. One of my favorites is Alfred, Julia and Carrie together. The

S. I. and Christine

girls had on matching dresses with velvet cuffs and white lace collars that I had made. I believe I made those collars detachable since they were so easy to get dirty. At age twelve, going on thirteen, Alfred's suit only fit him a short time before he started growing into puberty. Their angelic (and clean) looks were frozen in time in this picture.

Christine and S. I.'s wedding picture was taken at Atherton's in Salina since they were married there. In 1889, the bride wore her best dress, not a special white one that became popular later on.

She was the first child to live on the prairie and the first to leave home in this family. I always worried I'd lose her in the tall prairie grass when we first homesteaded, but never to growing up. After starting her American life in a primitive dugout, she now lives in a modern home in Salina. Their daughter, Anna, married four years ago and lives in Lindsborg.

After adventures in the Oklahoma land rush and the rugged hills of California, Willie came home, married neighbor girl, Minnie Granquist, and settled in as a Lindsborg area farmer and father of two girls, Martha and Viola. His sense of adventure continued though when he bought one of the first automobiles in the area in 1910.

Willie's family in front of their house

Alfred met Danish immigrant Marie Nelson at a dance in Bridgeport and they quietly married in our parlor in '02. Stair-stepping aged children with the ever-faithful dog ending the line-up portrays this family in front of their Hedville farm house.

Carrie was smitten with Per Sjogren at an early age and married in our parlor in 1896. Since the Sjogren farm was just down the road, I saw them often when the two little girls were small. In '03,

Alfred and Marie and family

Per, Carrie, Myrtle and Verna

they moved to the farm we purchased by Bavaria, then moved again to a farm near Smolan. When Myrtle married last summer, she and her husband, Frank Zachariason, took over the farm and Carrie and Per moved to Salina.

Julia was the first child of mine and Peter's new family. She almost could have been a grandchild since Christine was 22 when Julia was born. Life changed back to diapers again. She was also one of the easiest to raise because of her quiet temperament.

Joe and Julia's wedding picture

Her wedding took place here eight years ago. After nearly having her heart broken by an area boy, it was mended and healed solid by Peter Olson's son,

Axel and Mabel

19

Joe. Peter, my cousin, and Hannah, his wife and their children were our next door neighbors. Since both family's children were about the same ages, they were playmates since birth. When Joe and Julia were married, Peter and Hannah moved to Assaria and left the farm for the couple to take over.

If Julia is to be considered my most quiet child, Mabel, my last daughter is definitely the most rambunctious. She still goes full speed ahead and enjoys life. She would have had the guts to be a pioneer, but has had a very easy life instead. She gets more post-cards from boyfriends than all the girls of the township combined. She seems to be settling down and seeing Axel Linn a lot lately. He is very calm and quiet in contrast to her nature, but the difference seems to make a balanced couple.

Staring at the faded portrait of my parents, I have as much trouble remembering their aged faces as the photographer had at printing this copy. Their dark clothes can be seen in a sitting poise, but from their shoulders up, just an outline of their faces shows. I wish I had a better picture of them. They both died 37 years ago, just a few months apart. Oh, but I can still vividly recall my mother's face the day they finished their migration from Sweden and arrived at our homestead.

"Kaaaa-jsa. Kaaaa-jsa."

I stop working in the dugout and listen again. A person is attuned to the sounds of the prairie when they are alone, and that wasn't the wind blowing through the grass. The sound is closer. Ah!! Are they here? Are they here?! Even though my knees feel suddenly weak, I push my way around the primitive table in our dugout and rush out the door. Scaling the roof with a few giant bounds I turn to the direction the sound is coming from. My name is being called again! But by whose voice? I don't recognize the tenor voice, although it sounds familiar. I see them! Just barely visible above the tall grass I can see Carl and our wagon coming into sight in the far distance. The voice must be coming from the young man standing up in the back wagon, waving his hat. It must be Andrew's voice that has changed over the past years since I last saw him. My parents and other brother, Erick, are also in the wagon!

20

Grabbing Christina as she wanders out of the dugout, I roughly scoop her up, tuck the squirming two-year-old under my arm and run pell mell toward the wagon.

Even though I was sobbing, gasping for air and seeing through tear-filled eyes at the time, I can still picture the look on my mother's face when I reached the wagon. It was a look of sheer joy that her family was united again.

My family homesteaded on three claims to the south of us. Slowly their farms took shape as ours did. It made life so much easier to have family just down the road instead of across the ocean.

Erick married Magdalena Olson, our cousin and Peter Olson's sister, in 1883. Their marriage was blessed with Emelia, Hulda and Martin before it was cut short when Erick died of pneumonia five years later. Magdalena later remarried to Nels Johnson, her hired man, and had two more sons, Arthur and Elmer. When Arthur married Lillie Mattson this spring, Magdalena and Nels moved to Lindsborg so the newlyweds could live on the farm.

Andrew married Maria Petersson in '81 and had a daughter, Millie. I'll never forget the bad February blizzard in '12 during which Andrew died. He had been sick for about three weeks, and the weather did not help his recovery. The blizzard was so long and furious that the roads were blocked solid for quite a while, hampering the funeral. Star school was closed for two weeks. Most of the telephone poles and lines in the area were broken. We were set back in time, shut off from the world like our first years here.

My sisters stayed in Chicago and worked for a while before progressing on to Kansas. Emma married Frank Fager and farmed nearby until they moved to Lindsborg in '03 and then to California in '09.

Sara married Claus Sjogren, has four surviving children and lives near Smolan. Claus died two years also this coming November.

Our album contains photos of the family in their best clothes for all the special events in our lives—a new addition to the family, confirmations, weddings, and even sometimes death.

Present time has passed on as I went back into time looking at photos. Peter and Mabel have already retired to bed and I should go also.

When I turn down the wick on the lantern to put out the light, I'm pitched into blackness. Sitting here until my eyes adjust, I think of one photo I wish I had—one of my first husband, Carl Swenson. Not so much for me, but for our children and grandchildren. If I can't remember my parents well, I'm sure they don't remember him at all—except for that final memory.

Christina was ten years old when it happened; Willie, seven; Alma, four; Alfred, two; and I was pregnant with Carrie.

Rumble, rumble, a drum-rolling roar and a crescending crack that pierced the eardrums. Pouring rain, and then all of life stopped.

"Kajsa! Kajsa!", she screams at the top of her lungs. My mother-in-law's screeching voice and her panic stumbling toward our house makes fear and adrenalin rush through my veins. Before she reaches the end of the garden she collapses, sobbing that her son is dead.

"Which son?!" I whisper back, as morbid fear races through my body.

Svärmor is incoherent with shock and just keeps mumbling. "He and Mabry were walking home from the north field in the storm. Mabry was carrying a pitch fork across his shoulder. Lightning hit and killed them both!"

Oh my God! Carl, her oldest son—and my husband— was with Mabry!

Then there was darkness, and I never wanted to wake up.

Monday, July 21st

Life seems almost back on schedule this morning. We always wash on Monday and iron on Tuesday. I thought about waiting a day or so and doing some packing first, but then I'd really feel out of sync for the rest of the week. Technically it's no sin to wash on a Tuesday or Wednesday, but if a neighborhood woman went by and saw my clothes hanging on the line on a wrong day, she would probably stop by to see if I had been sick on Monday.

When the children were growing, I washed my clothes in a big iron kettle over an outside fire. It took all day to heat the water, dip and rub the clothes, rinse more than once and hang to dry.

Now I've got lighter metal washtubs to make washing easier. Two tubs are sitting on the low bench just outside the south door of the summer kitchen. During the summer we use the stove in the summer kitchen for as many things as possible to keep the kitchen from heating up. When we added on to this room, we lined up the stove so it could use the same chimney as the dining room stove on the opposite side of this wall. Right now the big wash boiler is filled with water and sitting across two burners. While waiting for the water to heat to almost boiling, I shave homemade lye soap into a bowl of hot water to soften up.

Making soap is a job I've always detested. I hate to work around lye fumes. I was sure one of the children would get burned by either the fire or the lye when they were little. I save ashes all year to make lye. After we butcher in the fall, the fat is cooked with the lye to make soap. After it hardens, the soap is cut in blocks, wrapped in cloth or straw, and stored in the cellar. I've always tried to make enough at one time to last a whole year.

Mabel sorts the clothes by color. Whites are always washed first; men's overalls last. She has helped with that job since she was about four years old. We'd make a game of it to learn colors and count the number of socks in a pile. There were enough socks to be washed for our family of nine that she could work on her multiplication tables.

Rather than lift the boiler off the stove, I bail the steaming hot water out with a small bucket, step out the south door and pour it into the wash tub. I still work outside if the weather allows. With the wooden laundry paddle, I mix the softened soap into the water, then add the first load of clothes. While we wait for the near boiling water to soak and soften the dirty clothes, Mabel goes to the well and refills two buckets of water to replace what I've taken out of the boiler. From this side of the summer kitchen, its just thirty steps to the well.

Dirty water from the wash tubs will dipped out with a bucket and thrown on the flower beds. Water from such jobs is always saved and used somewhere. It is too precious and too much work to draw it from the well without using it wisely.

After swirling the clothes in the water with the paddle, I stick the wash board down the inside of the tub. Gingerly testing the water to make sure it has cooled a bit, I pull the first shirt out of the water and scrub it with the palm of my hand on the board. When the spots are gone, I hold the collar between the two rollers of the wringer that is clamped on the side of the tub and Mabel turns the crank that pulls the shirt through the smooth rollers and presses the water out of the material. It sure beats wringing out the clothes by hand. I always got painful cramps in my hands and wrists after washing and rinsing clothes for the whole family.

Mabel fills the next tub with clear cold water and rinses the first load. Going through the wringer again, the clothing is put into a third tub of clear water in which bluing has been added to whiten the fabric. By now sweat is pouring down my face, even though it is still early morning. The steam from the hot water feels like it could melt my skin at times.

During the winter I usually do the wash in the summer kitchen. If there is plenty of water in the cistern on the back porch, I use that water instead of trampling out in the snow to the well. Clothes still need to be hung on the line. Wiping the line with a vinegar-soaked rag keeps the clothes from freezing to the line. The freeze-dried pieces of clothing are as stiff-as-a-board when they are first brought in. Then they melt into a damp pile. Thinking about winter washing cooled down my thoughts for a little while.

Mabel lugs the heavy basket of wet clothes over to the line for me and then goes back to the summer kitchen to start the process of washing the next load. Walking through the summer kitchen, I lift the clothespin bag off its nail on the side of the wall, and automatically fill my apron pocket with pins as I walk to the line. The clothesline, which is actually a set of three wires, running parallel west and east and attached to poles at both ends, is on the north side of the house, away from the dust of the road and yard. Hooking the bag on the middle wire at one end, I rub a wet rag along the clothes line first to get the bird droppings off the wire. Out of habit, I start on the east end of the farthest line and throw the shirts across the wire, about three feet apart. Pulling the first shirt off the line, I snap it to get the wrinkles out and pin it upside down with two pins. The breeze catches the center of the shirt and it becomes an anchored sail in the wind. Now just taking one pin from my pocket, I repin the second shirt corner over the first shirt corner, then put the second pin on. This way you only use half as many clothespins and the clothes make a stronger front against the wind. Every now and then the wind gets too strong, a piece of clothing is tugged off the line and you end up washing the item again.

Through the flapping clothes I see Peter trudging up to the house. He takes his hat off and wipes his brow with a handkerchief he pulled out of his back pocket. He also blows his nose before stuffing the wet cloth back into its usual space. Swedish farmers always take a break every forenoon for coffee and something to eat. I'd worry, knowing something must be wrong if he didn't show up. After we get settled in town, what's he going to do with his time before forenoon lunch?

Peter has been going through the piles of tools and parts that have accumulated in the west room of the granary, sorting out things he wants to sell or pass on to the children's farms. I'm sure he'll be lost for a while after we move, but other interests in town activities will eventually fill the gap. I'll still have the laundry, cooking and cleaning to take care of, so I won't run out of things to do.

Not wanting to sit in the hot kitchen, we bring our cups of coffee and a container of sugar cookies out to the south porch. We sit in silence for a while. Although he doesn't say anything, the coffee must be too hot. Peter pours the coffee into his saucer to spread the liquid around to cool a bit. In the meantime he reaches for another handful of cookies.

A cookie crumb sticks to his mustache and I motion to my own face to show him what side the crumb is on. We know each other's language and he wipes it off without saying anything. He looks so tired. The emotional stress of this week lines his forehead. The stress will climax Thursday when the farm will be crowded with friends and strangers alike for the sale.

I have a few stains I need to take care of before this last load of clothes, so I rise and go to the kitchen. I don't have all day to do the laundry. I need to start packing this afternoon.

Men's clothing are always a challenge to keep clean because of what they get into. I rub butter into the axel grease stain smeared across the back of a work shirt. I no longer ask how in the world it got there. Rust, probably from going through all the old junk in the pile behind the coal house, stains yet another shirt. Cutting an onion in half, I rub one part on the rust spot. The other half of the onion I'll use for dinner today.

Back outside, I add these two shirts to the water and start scrubbing the last tub of clothes I'll wash on this farm.

The splash of the cool water on my face refreshes me for a little bit. The wash basin sits on the end of the work table that is fitted against the east wall, between the steps into the kitchen and the stove. A bucket and dipper have always sat in the same spot on the counter beside it. Everyone uses this area to clean up, whether it is a whole threshing crew coming in from the field for the noon meal or brushing one's teeth before going to bed. Wiping the water I dripped on the table with my towel, I look around the summer kitchen.

26

This section was first a porch off the back kitchen door. Then we enclosed it and added a small window and the north door. It is just a simple door of wood slates, with a diagonal board across the back to hold it together.

This is the only door in the house that doesn't have a door knob. Instead you push down on the metal piece with your thumb to raise the latch. That raises the bar that slips out of groove that is fastened to the inside of the door casing. Unfortunately someone lost the key so we couldn't lock the door. Peter added a small block of wood that turns on a nail to keep the door from being opened from the outside at night.

Later on we doubled the size of the room by extending it as far south as we could and added another window and a door with two panels of glass in the top. The lean-to roof slopes to the west. Shelves run across the whole length of this wall.

It is definitely a catch-all room. Manure-caked boots, that should have been scraped better before they came into the house, sit under a row of old coats hanging behind the north door. The chamber pot has been emptied from the night before and sits in its usual place until it is carried back into the bedroom this evening. The shotgun has always hung above the door, ready to be used at a moment's notice. The big 10-gallon butter churn sits in the corner. With only three of us at most meals, I use the gallon glass churn that sits on the shelf instead. Big utensils like the boiler, roaster and meat grinder sit on these shelves rather than take up space in the kitchen.

Everyday chores like separating the cream from the milk are done twice a day in this room. Eggs are candled to see if they are fertile, and then buffed clean and cased to be brought into town to be traded at the general store.

Many newborn calves have spent their first night in the summer kitchen by the stove when an early blizzard threatened their lives. I also think more than once an abandoned duckling cheeped in a box and was hand-fed oatmeal by the children.

The distinct smell of sunshine-dried clothing fills the air in the summer kitchen. Mabel hangs the clothespin bag back on its nail by the door as she hauls the dried garments into the room. I hope we remember to take the bag with us Friday.

Later on today, we will sprinkle the clothing with water and roll them up. Tomorrow morning after breakfast, Mabel will set up the ironing board near the stove, heat the sadirons on the stove's surface and iron today's wash.

Apparently the crumbling of the newspaper and clanking of the good china isn't bothering the two little ones taking their nap in my bed. Julia came over this afternoon after dinner to help Mabel and me pack the good dishes we used yesterday. She timed her arrival so her children would be ready for their afternoon nap. We'll get the fragile dishes packed first, before they wake up and want to help.

We pulled the dining room table closer to the china cabinet on the north wall to alleviate steps. The cabinet's doors gape open. The shelves have been unloaded of their stacks. Dishes, cups, saucers and various bowls wait on the table to be wrapped and packed into boxes and bushel baskets. Embroidered tea towels, flour sacks, shirts, petticoats and about everything else I could think of is piled on a chair to be used as layers to cushion my dishes for their trip into town. This is a tedious job, but I want every cup to arrive safely. We're not moving far, but one big bump on the road could make a basket full of china fragments if not packed right.

Everything in the dining room and parlor can be packed today. My everyday dishes must wait until the end of the week since we have several more meals to cook and eat here.

I'm not being very modest, but as I reach for the dish on top of the piano, I realize I'm proud of the parlor. My best has always been displayed here, whether it be chairs, dishes or knickknacks. Many items are gifts from the children. The first presents the children gave me were crude, handmade items, made from things they found outdoors or of scraps in the house. Those are some of the most treasured gifts I have. Later on, I received more expensive presents as they could afford it. Even though I protested, I felt pride in them being able to give such things to me. All these treasures will move with me and find a new place to be admired from.

A trunk has been emptied of it quilts into the corner of the parlor. The trunk is refilled with the photo albums and things that have graced the top of the piano and parlor table. The lamp will have to sit there until Friday morning since we still need it to light the room. We'll have to empty the kerosene from the bottom glass before we pack it. The top can be wrapped in the piano runner and the parlor pillows stuffed around it in the trunk to protect it. We will have electricity in town, but we'll keep the lamp out so we're prepared if the power fails. We will move the table and chairs as is, but I want the quilts to be wrapped around them so they don't rub against something and get damaged.

Quilts. Multi-colorful patches of material that keep us warm during the cold winter months. I wonder how many quilts I've made in my lifetime. Sometimes the quilt stand has stood up in the parlor for months with quilts in progress. Besides being needed for beds here, we made quilts for all the girls' new homes. They may have been stitched together here, but now the quilts are scattered and keeping loved ones warm everywhere.

The best material scraps were saved for the quilts. Cut into particular pieces for a pattern, like the wedding bands design or used as is for a crazy patchwork pattern, hours were spent hand stitching the pieces into the top. Then the backing fabric, middle batting for layered warmth and the top are tacked together and stretched onto the quilt frame. We would quilt together whenever we had time to spend on the project. Quite often, we would have a quilting bee and invite neighborhood women to help. When you had several women quilting on each side of the frame at once, the quilt could be finished in a few days instead of weeks that it would take one or two people.

During the homesteading days when women rarely left the township, getting together to work on someone's quilt was a God-send. We needed each other's company almost more than a helping hand with a needle. If the quilting bee fell on a day of nice weather, it more than likely was held outside. There was much more room and better light than inside the dark dugout. Usually you had to bring your own chair or stool, because the hostess only had a few in her sparse home.

My basket of embroidery work beside the rocker can just as well be packed. I won't have time to work on any projects this week. Women's hands are never idle. Now I just do fancy work for gifts and to keep my fingers nimble.

I made our clothing—from our underwear to our coats—and knitted our socks and hats. When I wasn't making or altering clothing, I'd tear old material into strips, sew the long pieces together and roll the long bands of color around each other into a large ball. When I had enough wrapped balls, the strips were braided into a wide flat band and sewn together to form oval rag rugs.

When I was a child in Sweden, my mother had a loom. We raised our own sheep for wool; sheared, washed, carded and spin the wool into yarn before threading it on the loom and weaving the material for our clothing. She used this same method to make her rugs. Strips of worn out material were given new life by being bound together for strength. Her rugs were always rectangular in shape.

I remember the living room had long strips of rugs running almost the entire length of the room. The widest width strip her loom made was three feet, so she had four strips laying side by side, sewn together on the margins. Thinking how long it would take to save that many strips of material, I realize it was added onto several times before it got to its finished size.

While my mother and I did sewing because we had to clothe our family, Alma and Julia professionally sewed for people around the neighborhood before they married. By then, farms were prospering and the farm women could afford to have help in sewing clothing for their large families. In those years, sewing projects seemed to take over the dining room and parlor at times. Beautiful formal gowns, tailored men's suits and simple children's clothing started out as material being cut out on the dining room table. Both girls pumped miles on the treadle sewing machine and hand-stitched hundreds of tiny tucks and pleats onto outfits.

Of course some of the best work was done on their own wedding gowns. Alma's white dress had hundreds of little pleats and minute details. She finished her ensemble with a cloud of tulle that crowned her bright blonde hair and trailed all the way down her back to the floor.

When Julia married eleven years later, fashion styles had changed. She made a tailored, cream-colored linen and silk gown. It had three-quarter length sleeves and she wore elbow length gloves with it. Instead of a veil, two white gardenias were tucked in her hair. The flowers matched her groom's boutonniere.

Whenever I think of Joe and Julia's wedding, I always think of the interruption we had during the ceremony. While they were saying their vows, the telephone rang. Rather than to let it keep ringing, someone went back into the dining room and answered it. Mr. Trulson from the Assaria elevator was calling to tell Peter that wheat had reached a dollar a bushel. "Did he want to sell?" Of course Peter took the phone call to say yes, they would deliver the wheat tomorrow since they were "kind of" busy today with their daughter's wedding. The new groom was busy the next day too, because he helped Peter deliver the loads of wheat to the elevator.

There isn't much to pack in the small bedroom between the parlor and our bedroom. Because of the window and two doors taking up wall space, there is only a single bed, a small wash stand and chair in here. This little 8 by 8 foot room served as the first bedroom for several of the children. The room served as a regular bedroom when Peter's father stayed with us a while. Anders was confined to a wheelchair most of the time. Since the little room opened into the parlor, it was a perfect setup for him. Other older friends and relatives that didn't wish to climb the narrow stairs to the upstairs bedroom have used the room too.

The other door in the little bedroom leads into the area that is below the stair landing upstairs. It is mainly used as a passageway between the parlor, little room and our bedroom. A three-foot high door opens to a small closet underneath the stairs. It holds suitcases, hat boxes and occasionally a hiding child.

"Want to go for a drive?," asks Peter after supper.

I had planned to go through our bedroom dresser drawers this evening, but the invitation to drive around our township is more inviting. Today's heat and high humidity has made the house almost unbearable and any excuse to get out in the breeze sounds good. I don't bother to change. I just take off my apron and grab my straw hat. We don't plan to stop any place, so I don't need my good hat and gloves.

Peter hesitates at the driveway, deciding which way to go first. Making up his mind, he heads south on the dirt road. Hedge rows, running along weed-filled ditches, line the road. Our south field is divided into three sections by the hedge. Looking between the trees I get glimpses of different crops growing in the field. Straight green stalks of corn, about ready to tassel in a week or so, is in the first section. A few very early starts of tassels can be seen poking up above the leaves. Faded yellow wheat stubble, with a few dark green weeds mixed in, wait for fall plowing in the middle patch. Purple-dotted perennial alfalfa lines the patch closest to the creek. It has been cut and dried twice this summer. It looks like it is about ready to be cut again.

A variety of crops are grown in our community—wheat, oats, corn, sorghum and alfalfa. The farmers need a variety of grains to feed their livestock. In turn, the fatted steers are shipped by rail from the Hallville stockyards to Kansas City to be sold at the best price. Wheat is our other cash crop. What we don't use for seed wheat or ground for flour, is sold to the local elevator. We have such an excess of grain and livestock now. To think we started out planting a few bushels of wheat and corn the first year in the prairie sod we turned. Our survival on our new land depended on that seed. That first grain was so precious, we protected it like it was gold. Now we harvest thousands of bushels a year.

The same for livestock. We didn't have the money for a cow our first year. Finally Carl was able to trade work with the Robinsons for her. Last fall we shipped a rail car full of steers to market.

The large cottonwood trees along the creek in the south pasture loom ahead. Peter is driving about as slow was the car will go, so we can savor the view. Even at this slow pace, my mind flashes this same scene over and over, only in different time frames and seasons. Peter and I reminisce out loud to each other.

"Remember the time we went down to the pasture to check the cows and new calves and it was snowing so hard coming back that we had to follow the fence line, hand over hand, to find our way home?"

"What was the name of that thresher who had the runaway team that crashed the binding machine into the west hedge row?"

"How many men did we have camping in the south field when they built the railroad track through this area?"

We cross the bridge that spans the creek which runs through our pasture. At the moment there is no water flowing down the creek bed. The rustling of the cottonwoods is loud this evening. They are still shedding their cotton. It fills the air as it floats in the wind. The grass on the edge of the road has a drift of cotton in it that reminds me of snow.

The creek starts three sections to the southeast of here and flows into the river a mile north past our place. If we would get a hard three-inch rain tonight, the creek would rise and overflow faster than we could move. More than once we woke up to hear frog's croaking and the sound of rushing water working its way toward the house. Sometimes it would even flow down from the section to the east of us and across the road.

We pass the middle section line of fence that runs between our land and what my brother, Erick, homesteaded. The south 80 acres of this land was first homesteaded by my parents. They and Erick built a house together on the dividing line so it would count for both claims. Later they each built their own homes which have been expanded and remodeled over time.

Across the road to the east, the windmill at John and Emma Johnson's farm turns placidly in the breeze. John is Nels Johnson's brother and farms this 80 acres now. Nels Sjogren farmed it in the beginning. His son Per took over the farm when he married my Carrie. It was nice to have them so close. They later moved to the Bavaria farm that we bought and this farm changed hands again.

From the south intersection we can see Andrew and Emelia Swenson's new home they built last year. It is a huge two and a half story wood-frame home. So far, my niece's three little children don't fill up the big house. This is the farm where Minnie Granquist's parents lived until they moved to Lindsborg.

From this corner looking west, we can see a glimpse of the Smoky Hill Bluffs. Right now they have a grey hue to them. Their looks are ever changing depending on the time of day and the weather. When a person travels another mile south to a higher elevation, they can see the whole Smoky Hill valley spreading down to the river and then back up towards the bluffs.

I remember this view most vividly since this is where I stood by and watched my first husband's casket being lowered into the ground.

It was in this corner pasture, up on the hill, where we buried Carl and Mabry after their accident. Because of area flooding, we couldn't get to the Assaria cemetery, so the men were buried in my brother Andrew's pasture. It has been years since I visited the grave. It isn't marked, but I think I could walk right up to the spot. Peter sees that I'm searching for the graves by the way I'm craning my neck, so he stops and asks if I'd like to walk up to the site.

Parking the car along the side of the road, we cross the ditch to the four-wire fence. Gathering up my skirt, I lean through the gap of wire that Peter has pushed apart with his hand and foot and cross the fence. I hold the fence wire the same way for Peter so he can crawl through. Cows grazing at the top of the hill momentarily look up from chewing off grass to see what we're up to, then put their heads down for another bite. Clumps of tall blue stem mix in with the buffalo grass, yarrow and butterfly weed. This spring the pasture was a rich palette of greens, pinks and yellows with the wildflowers blooming. Summer heat in late July has turned the stems and seed pods to colors of light greens, browns and grays. Watching my steps through stickery plants, cow chips and rocks, I make my way up the hill. The breeze blows wisps of fine white hair into my eyes.

It is not so much I know the exact spot, but I can look back toward our farm and know when I'm at the right angle. I spent so much time up here at first, talking to Carl. It was such a heavy load trying to run the farm and take care of the children by myself. I just needed to talk to him. It seemed to help if I came up to his grave and asked the questions out loud. I even brought newborn Carrie up here to "meet" him. That was definitely the darkest period of my life.

Then Peter came looking for a job and I had someone to help me run the farm again. My trips to the grave decreased until Peter and I lost a daughter and we buried her up here beside Carl. She would have been 33 years old now if she had lived.

Leaning down over his grave, I touch the ground and whisper, "Carl, I'm leaving the homestead Friday. Will you watch over it for me?" Patting the ground, I rise and look back toward our farm. For some unexplained reason, I don't think I'll ever make it up here again. This was my final talk with Carl.

Heading back to the corner and turning east, we drive along the land that Andrew homesteaded. Part of his land is pasture, part fields and part a timber claim. Trees line the east fence before it breaks for the farmstead. The farmstead used to be in plain sight until the trees matured and surrounded the place. You have to cross a little creek at the first of the driveway to get to the house. Andrew lived here on the land for ten years before he met and married Maria. She traveled to America with Magdalena when she and her parents joined her brother, Peter Olson. Their first log home was eventually replaced with a two-story house, similar to ours. We've spent many happy family gatherings on this farm. I hope Millie and Anton keep up the tradition.

Driving on east we comment how farms have changed families over the decades. When we settled here, we could travel miles without seeing a tree, building or plowed field. Now there is an

Family gathering at Andrew Johnson's home

established farmstead surrounded by a ring of trees every 80 or 160 acres.

At the mile line looking south, we glimpse the Miller home. The land was first homesteaded by Peter Olson, but sold when they moved to Assaria for a short time to run the livery stable. After changing hands a time or two, Dan Miller and his family came from Tennessee and settled onto the land. His son, Nat, and his wife Pearl, farm the land now.

The Miller home

Driving on another mile we pass Mattson's land. We cross the creek again that flows by our place. Mattson's house sits right in the flood plain on the creek bank. They always have problems with flooding before it reaches us. Hannah's husband died at an early age and she raised nine children by herself. Now it is just Hannah and her sons, Carl and Philip, left at home since her daughter, Lillie, married Art Johnson. Yesterday at our women's meeting, Hannah mentioned she and Carl will move to Bridgeport next spring when Philip marries Ame Laessig.

A side-by-side four hitch team is pulling a riding two-bottom plow in the next section. Emil Fagerberg is getting an early start on plowing the wheat stubble on the Schippel land. Being a German Catholic bachelor, Emil doesn't associate with the Hallville Swedes very much and we rarely see him. But as we turn the corner and head north, he waves to acknowledge our passing car.

Wheeler School looms ahead on the next corner. It was built after Star School got too crowded and the district split. The two schools have always had a fun rivalry, sharing everything from ball games, music programs, to spelling bees.

Turning the car west, Peter puts up his arm to shield his eyes from the setting sun. He slows down as he passes Thomas and Hanna Olson's home. They rented my parents farm when they first lived in our community, so their children grew up with ours. Their four adult children, now in the thirties and forties, still live with them and run the farm. Looks like the boys are farming late tonight too. Swan is on the mower finishing a patch of alfalfa and Nels is running the hay rake over what was cut yesterday. The odor of green alfalfa leaves drifts over the area as we drive through it. I love the smell.

There goes their sisters, Hannah and Bessie, cutting across the field with a late supper. Bessie has a basket in the crook of her arm that contains the meal. Hannah carries the coffee pot wrapped in the towel. She is known for making the hottest coffee in the township. I don't know how she does it, but it is always scaling hot. When Hannah pours you a cup of coffee, you better let it cool a bit before taking the first sip. They worked for families in Salina in their early years before moving back to the farm. Now people hire the sisters to prepare wedding meals. They are both excellent cooks.

Across the road to the north is where my niece Hulda and her husband, Elof Peterson, live. Before the young couple married and moved into the house, Elof's parents, Louis and Jenny farmed the land. Elof's sister Lydia, married neighbor boy, Emil Carlson. His other sister, Emily, married Henry Trulson, but died in childbirth eight years ago.

Pete and Emma Almquist farm the land northwest of this intersection. Måns Peterson gave this quarter section to his daughter when she married Pete, his hired man. Although married a little late in life, they have a family of four sons and a daughter. Starting from scratch on native grass, they built a house, barn and established an acre of orchard trees that is the envy of the neighborhood. During good years, they sell their surplus of fruit. I usually get a couple of bushels of apricots from their trees each year since I don't grow that kind of tree.

The Elof Peterson home

Black smoke puffs from the smokestack and trails up in the air as the train gets ready to leave the Hallville Depot that runs through Almquist's land. The Missouri Pacific Line stops at this depot for water and supplies.

A town did not spring around this depot like most places on the prairie. Bridgeport, a few miles further west, was already established when the rail line was built. That's just fine with this farming community. It has served our needs. We can ship cattle out of the stock yards, store our wheat at the elevator until time to load onto rail cars, and get supplies at the general store. Our plow shares are sharpened and equipment repaired at the blacksmith shop. Mail was dropped off here for the community for years until it was absorbed into the Bridgeport route.

Emil Carlson, who grew up just south of Hallville corner, managed the store for years. Ola Peterson and his second wife, Kristina, took over the store and depot in '10. They and their five children live in the back part of the store. People stop in the store for news and conversation as much as for food or gasoline.

Ola and his nephew, Charlie Peterson, added the elevator five years ago. It has saved the farmers so much time since they can now haul their wheat to Hallville instead of Assaria.

Hallville Store

When our community decided to build a chapel about ten years ago, Hallville was the perfect choice. Pete and Emma Almquist donated part of their quarter section for the building site. It is a rather small building, by church standards, but it was what we could afford. It is furnished inside with simple wooden pews and seats about a hundred and fifty people. The one adornment in the chapel is the large altar oil painting depicting the Good Shepherd leading a flock of sheep. Pastor Erickson of the Assaria congregation holds service here every other Sunday afternoon. Before church, we divide up for Sunday School. The young children have lessons in the front, older children in the middle, and we old people have Swedish Bible study in the back pews. It is very noisy with the groups competing to be heard, but we'd much rather be crowded here than travel all the way to Assaria. With livestock chores to do in the morning, we didn't always make it to Assaria's morning service, so the Hallville Chapel has definitely filled a void in our spiritual needs.

We have two active auxiliary groups. The young people are active in their Luther League and we women meet regularly for our Women's Missionary Society.

My favorite time at Hallville Chapel is Christmas. The building overflows with people for our Christmas program. Latecomers end up standing in the back. The stove in the center of the room radiates

Hallville Chapel

Interior of Hallville Chapel

a cozy feeling as families come in from the dark, snowy night. The glow of lighted candles on the Christmas tree illuminates the tinsel cones and glass ornaments adoring the branches. Little children fuss in their Christmas velvet outfits as they sit in the front pews waiting their turn to recite their memorized Christmas verse. Eyeing the wicker laundry basket of apples and sacked candy in the front of the chapel, they know their reward will be hand delivered after the program. Everyone gets involved with singing Christmas hymns, both in English and our favorite old Swedish ones. We'll have to make it back to Hallville this Christmas.

Turning the corner north again, we comment on the Rames, Linn and Runberg farms situated at this crossroad. We all had children the same age in Star School. We all mourned together when some of their children died from sickness.

Anna Stenfors' farm sits on the hill to the west. John and wife, Goldie and their family tend the land now.

The east farm is Charlie Peterson's. He and Alma were married right after my Alma and Nels. Their six children play with Julia's children quite often since Alma Peterson and Joe are brother and sister.

The sun is starting to sink below the bluffs. Peter turns the car west at the next intersection to start home.

The Robinson estate. Laura Robinson Harne inherited the land, but hasn't lived on it since she married. The Albert Eagles family live in the big house and farm the land now.

Charlie Peterson's children

41

We spent so much time at the Robinson homestead when we first moved here. I remember when we first met Benjamin and Adelaide, and their hired man, Larry Lapsley. I don't know what we would have done without their help that first year. In exchange for Carl helping with their field work, they gave us our first seed for the fields and loaned us the plow to break the sod to plant it.

Mrs. Robinson was the only female for me to talk to at first. It was tough since I only spoke Swedish, but we managed to create a bond that lasted throughout the years.

The Robinsons were very active in the community, taking part in all the school responsibilities. Being English though, they were involved in the Bridgeport Church instead of the Swedish-speaking Assaria Church with us.

Their farm prospered. In their later years, when their daughter, Laura, married and moved to Salina, Benjamin and Adelaide moved into town during the winters, then almost year round when their health got worse. Their big house was closed up and sat empty until they came back to the community in the spring. They had a hired man and his family live in a small house on the farm to take care of the place.

Benjamin died ten years ago and was buried on their farm with other family members. Their two young sons, Adelaide's father and stepmother, and Mr. Lapsley preceded him in death. Adelaide died just this May at her daughter's home. We went to Salina for the funeral because she was buried in Salina instead of their farm.

Mr. Larry Lapsley. The Robinson's befriended the black slave during the Civil War after he escaped the South and walked to Kansas. He was a character and a bright spot on the prairie. Larry appreciated everything he had, no matter how limited his resources or possessions were. He homesteaded 80 acres along the creek a quarter mile west of here. Larry had heart trouble and died when he was in his 50s. His very modest home was moved to the Olson farm after he died. It's now used as a chicken house.

I wish I had a picture of him to show the grandchildren since they have heard so many tales about him. He was such an important person in our family and the whole community.

He loved children and spent many hours at Star School. He never missed a social event involving the children. Larry was a walking history lesson and the teachers welcomed him to talk to the pupils. He didn't learn to read or write until he settled in the area. I think his influence helped many students overcome their own problems.

Curving along the river, we head back south toward home, passing nephew Martin Johnson's farm. Years before them, the Rittgers lived there. Mr. Rittger died in '03 of malarial fever, leaving his wife with 12 children and the farm to take care of. I'm not sure where they live now.

When I stop to really think about it, the neighborhood has been changing constantly ever since we broke the first sod. Several of our first neighbors are still here, but they have lost a mate and their children have taken over the active management of the farm. Some families only rented land and moved on after a short period of time. Buildings have been built, torn down and replaced. Groves of trees and orchards have sectioned apart the endless sea of grass. Noises of automobiles now disrupt the air that could be perfectly quiet for hours back before the turn of the century.

The sun has dipped behind the western bluffs as we pass Joe and Julia's farm. The black outlines of the Olson house and out-buildings silhouette against the brilliant swirls of red and yellow that line the sky where the sun set a few minutes ago. Peter steps on the car's clutch to slow our travel and we coast slowly by their place. The soft glow of a lantern illuminates from a window in their house. I imagine Julia is rocking one of the children asleep. I wonder which lullaby she is singing tonight. Is it the old Swedish one that my mother sang to me?

The belfry of the school house points upward to the prairie sky as we pass the school. I'll miss the morning ringing of the school bell this fall.

Darkness has settled into our own farm as we pull into the driveway. Mabel is out with friends tonight, so the house is dark and alone; just like it will be at the end of the week.

Another day has ended in our last week on the farm.

Tuesday, July 22nd

The doorway to the attic is on a inward slant, because of the roof line, and opens in two sections. The weight of the top door drops against my waiting lifted left arm as my right hand turns the wooden bar on the nail that holds the top door up. After swinging it downward and out of the way, I pull the peg out of the hole that holds the bottom half shut and open the door. Bright specks of dust dance in the air as light beams through the little dirty window at the end of the room. A cloud of dust penetrates my nostrils and make my teeth gritty since I disturbed the dust layer on the doors I just opened.

I want to clean out this room first thing this morning before the heat rises and makes it unbearable to be in here. Never finished, the dark unplastered wall and roof boards let in the hot or cold depending on the season.

Darker than normal stains on the ceiling show that rain has leaked through the roof around the chimney again.

As is true for most storage spaces, the attic is full of boxes, odds and ends, old furniture—a scattering of items that have been important at some point in our lives. Things I've totally forgot we own until I spy them again.

The room could easily be considered cluttered. It's easy to open the door, add something else to the pile on top of a trunk, with honest intentions of packing them away tomorrow. But you close the door and sometimes forget what you do not see.

A delicate cobweb gingerly hangs by a thread from the top of the window sill to an ancient buffalo robe coat that hasn't been disturbed for a decade. I remember it used to be a dark brown, but now with the permanent creases filled with dust, it has taken on a light gray shade.

I'm in the habit of never throwing something away that could be used again. Empty wooden spools strung together on a string hang on a nail. They have been used for everything from rewrapping saved thread to hammering a nail through its hole and using it as a wall hook.

Toys of the past. Rusty ice skates hang on a nail from one of the rafters. Handmade wooden stilts rest in the left corner. A wooden crate houses a crude bat and baseball. They spent hours outside playing with those toys. Now they lay neglected and forgotten.

The oldest children had very few toys since we couldn't afford anything but homemade. Christine made do with her imagination her first years since there were no playmates nearby either. Carl and I made a little rag doll with a wooden head that she dragged everywhere.

Mabel's pencil scribbling on the top of one box identifies it as from the children's school days at Star. Shifting through the graded papers, I realize most of them are Julia's and Mabel's. The older children, especially Christine and Willie, used small blackboard slates to do their lessons on. Paper, or the money to buy the paper, was scare then. Lifting out the pile of papers, I find the bumps beneath the stack are a variety of articles—short stubby hand-whit-tled pencils, quill pens, a dried up bottle of ink, a red hair ribbon and a grade card from 1888.

There are two books in the box, one very small, for little hands to hold, and a large one. I reach for the schoolbook, *ABC eller Barnens Första Bok för Skolan och Hemmet.* (*ABC or The Childrens First Book for the School and the Home.*) The cardboard cover and green cloth spine show wear from much use. All seven of my children used this book, plus most of the children in the neighborhood. Books were scare when we started the school back in 1874 and all the students shared the same few books the school board could buy, beg or borrow.

The final item in the bottom of the box is a black leather book. Oh goodness, it is the first record book of Star School. After this first book's pages were filled, it was set aside and a new book

Oaths of Office.

I do solemnly Swear (or Affirm,) That I will support the Constitution of the United States, and the Constitution of the State, and that I will faithfully discharge the duties of the office of _Director_ of School District, No. _46_ County of _Saline_ according to the best of my ability. So help me God.   _B. S. Robinson_

Saline COUNTY,

I DO HEREBY CERTIFY That the foregoing Oath was taken and subscribed to by the said _B. S. Robinson_ before me this _13_ day of _August_ A. D. 18_74_   _C. E. Lamkin_

I do solemnly Swear (or Affirm,) That I will support the Constitution of the United States, and the Constitution of the State, and that I will faithfully discharge the duties of the office of _Clerk_ of School District, No. _46_ County of _Saline_ according to the best of my ability. So help me God.   _Chas. B. Wheaton_

Saline COUNTY,

I DO HEREBY CERTIFY That the foregoing Oath was taken and subscribed to by the said _C. B. Wheaton_ before me this _13_ day of _August_ A. D. 18_74_   _C. E. Lamkin_

I do solemnly Swear (or Affirm,) That I will support the Constitution of the United States, and the Constitution of the State, and that I will faithfully discharge the duties of the office of _Treasurer_ of School District, No. _46_ County of _Saline_ according to the best of my ability. So help me God.   _Robert Wheeler_

Saline COUNTY,

I DO HEREBY CERTIFY That the foregoing Oath was taken and subscribed to by the said _Robert Wheeler_ before me this _11_ day of _August_ A. D. 18_74_   _C. E. Lamkin_

started. Peter must have been treasurer of the district that year, so it just stayed here. Leafing through the book brings back memories of the start of the school, and the people who founded it. One of the first pages filled out is the "Oaths of Office," dated August 13, 1874.

Signatures of B. F. Robinson, Chas. O. Wheaten, C. E. Lamkin and Robert Wheeler stare back at me. These men are all gone now.

The book had pages to fill out for the teachers employed, teacher's contracts, and annual meeting reports. Carl's signature is on the August 10th, 1876 minutes. He was the secretary of the board that year. He wrote the minutes in English, but there are several Swedish words mixed in.

It's been 45 years since we started the school. We had several families living in the township by then and we knew the children needed to be educated to prosper in our new country. We donated an acre of land on the corner of our farm since we were centrally located. The Lone Star School became the center of the community and we never regretted giving up land for it. Even after our children graduated from Star, our lives have still revolved around the school. Besides school, many literary meetings, Grange discussions and church services were regularly held in the building. For a number of years, the whole neighborhood met at the school for a gigantic Thanksgiving meal.

The shape of the *ljuskrona* hides under a sheet in one corner. It is the oldest Christmas decoration we have, and the most important as far as our Swedish and family traditions. No matter their age, my oldest children always insisted the candles be lit each Christmas Eve on this candelabra, in remembrance of their father. Carl carved the ljuskrona out of wood from the river for our very first Christmas on the prairie. It started out with three branches. He added another branch for each new child. After Carl died and Carrie was born, his branch became hers.

In the same corner is the crate simply marked "Christmas." After St. Knuts Day ends the Christmas season, the tree decorations are carefully packed away for the next season, so they don't need to be packed again, but I peek into the ornament box anyway. Unwrapping one ball of tissue paper reveals a gold glass bell. Unwrapping again I marvel at the crude star fashioned out of sticks and red yarn. Delicate hand-blown glass ornaments are mixed in with crude, hand-made ones of my children and grandchildren. Each has a story behind it and I could never part with any of them.

The smell of must and old preserving herbs drifts toward my nose as I lift the heavy lid on one trunk.

Carefully folded on top are the white dresses the girls wore for their church confirmations. At a budding age the dresses didn't fit for very long, but they were important for the event and we spent hours hand-sewing lace trim on each one.

Most dresses I made were worn by all the girls. As Christine grew too big for a particular dress, Alma wore it next and so on. Sometimes the dresses was passed on to younger neighborhood girls too. Originally I made the children's clothing by cutting apart my old dresses and remaking them to fit their needs. On a few special occasions, I'd buy a whole bolt of material and all the girls would have matching outfits. Eventually the children's clothes were retired and became part of a quilt top.

The tiny yellowed christening dress worn by all my children was never destined for a rag or quilt. First worn by Christine in Sweden, I packed it for the trip to America because I hoped we'd have more children. Willie, Alma and Alfred wore it when they were baptized by the Salemsborg pastor. After we started the Assaria Church, Carrie, Julia and Mabel were baptized into that congregation. It was wrapped in my mother's favorite woolen shawl that she wore when she arrived here from Sweden.

I have fifty years worth of keepsake items stuffed away in trunks. We were just married when we moved to America and hadn't started to accumulate many things yet. Think of all the keepsake treasures my mother had to leave behind when they left Sweden! They had been married over 30 years. But I'm sure she was glad she followed her family to America rather than sit in her attic and stare at a trunkload of clothes.

Where are my letters from Sweden? Surely I kept the letters we received from our families when we first moved to America. Each one was sacred, a cherished link to our family across the water. They were read and re-read so many times, I can still remember parts of them. Did I burn them after our families arrived here? I didn't need the pieces of paper anymore to feel close to them, but now it would be nice to touch them again, read them to the grandchildren who never met their great-grandparents. Maybe I'll still find them as I go through things.

I lay my hand on the trunk that traveled with us when we left Sweden. At the time I agonized over what few essential and precious items would make the trip in this small chest. Tools on the bottom, a minimal amount of clothing and bedding, our church transfer papers, the *Svensk Pslambok*, family Bible and a few other essentials were all that would fit in the trunk. I packed our food supply in a huge basket, and Carl kept our savings and the key to the trunk on him at all times. I can't believe how little we brought to America. Now look at all the discarded things in this room. Think how much easier it would be to travel again if I didn't have 50 years worth of things to sift through and move!

On one wall is a stack of old pictures and frames that have hung in our rooms at various times. One of my favorites, that the children didn't seem to understand, is a print of the Swedish royal family. My ties have always been strong with my old country, but these people don't mean anything to my American-born children. The family members are identified at the bottom on the print. I turn it over to find a date, but don't see any. I set the picture back down, the glass facing the wall to protect it from getting hit when we start moving the boxes out.

Everything has been sorted through. Some things we don't want and we'll sell Thursday; the rest will go with the first load to our new house in town. We thought it would be best to start at the top of our house, clean it out and move it to the top of our next house to keep both houses from utter chaos.

When we added onto the house, Christine and Alma moved into the south bedroom, above the parlor. Eventually Carrie moved up from the little room when Julia was born, then Mabel.

Starting from three feet from the floor, the ceiling pitches in on the west and east as it follows the roof line. We plastered and papered the walls, but just painted the ceiling boards white. Beds and dressers had to be arranged where they would fit. Instead of a closet, clothes hang on hooks that line the straight walls. Rugs cover the floor to muffle the sound of feet and to add some warmth. One window faces south.

During the coldest months of the year, the room was used only for sleeping since there was no heat upstairs. Every morning the children would race downstairs to dress in front of the warm stove.

During really hot summer nights, the porch was the favored sleeping spot instead of the stuffy upstairs.

Being the girls' room, possessions and priorities changed in this room as they grew older. Make-believe conversations with dolls changed to talks about boys. Changing figures meant concern for the body and stylish clothes. Straggly pigtails changed to upswept chignons.

Standing at the foot of the stairs I could sometimes hear whispers in the night, secrets they didn't think I knew. Other times soft crying or open sobs drifted downstairs and filled the house. Either they had been reprimanded for doing something wrong at home or school, or a sibling or friend had hurt their feelings. The older sisters had to be careful about their gossip because there was always a younger sister ready to spread it around the neighborhood. Depending on what combination of sisters lived in this room, it was either neat-as-a-pin or helter skelter.

Mabel is the only one left in the room now. Her photo albums are piled on her bed. I imagine she was looking at them until late last night. It looks like she put them on the floor to sleep in the bed and then piled them on top again. The bed covers are not made under the albums. Mabel has a portable camera and snaps pictures everywhere she goes, whether it is on a young people's picnic at Soldier's Cap Mound, or around the farm. She records the life of our family.

The room definitely has Mabel's flare now. Favorite photos and postcards are stuck between the wood frame and glass of the dresser mirror. Ornate glass perfume bottles line the dresser scarf behind the laid out brush and hand mirror set. The latest fashion magazines vie for space on the small desk with souvenirs from her trips to visit Illinois cousins. The poor curtain, which I just washed and ironed last week, is tied up in a knot and pinned to the top curtain rod with a hat pin. Either she is trying to get more breeze through the window or the curtain was blocking her view of who was coming down the road from the south.

I think I'll let her worry about getting this room packed up by herself. She'll probably put it off until Thursday night.

As I rotate the white porcelain door knob of the small middle bedroom, I have to jerk the door slightly because it sticks at the top.

Only about 6 feet by 11 feet, this narrow room, with an inward slanting ceiling, has a window facing east at the far end and very little space. A small high shelf on the two foot space beside the window that has a straight wall, is loaded with a variety of textbooks each fall and is emptied again in April. All this room has usually contained is a single bed, dresser, and a teacher during the school year.

Although the Star School teacher has rotated to different homes in the neighborhood, they have customarily boarded with us since we are the closest house to the school building. We've had a variety of young schoolmarms and masters living with us over the years. Some of the young people became part of the family and came back for visits. Others just bid their time so they could leave this district for a larger school. They weren't interested in sharing their lives with us. When all seven children were still at home, it would have been nice to have had that room for part of our brood, but it was our way to help supply an education for the children of our township.

I recline on the bed in the north bedroom a moment to take a breather. The heat of the day is starting to warm the room.

Situated at the top of the stairs, this room, and our bedroom below it, was added on in the early '80s. This is the only upstairs room that has two windows. With one you get the view of the road. The other faces the railroad tracks to the north. It was Willie and Alfred's bedroom first. When all the older children moved out into their own homes, the two youngest finally had rooms of their own. Julia picked the north bedroom after Alfred married.

And to think four of us lived in space smaller than this room when we lived in the dugout. Now the room is used when we have family or friends visit, which seems to be fairly often. Our home has always been open and welcome to others.

Many a nap has been taken up here by a grandchild too. Do they dream the same dreams their parents did when they slept in this bed or stared at the ceiling waiting for sleep to take over their weary minds? Adventures of sailing the salt-water sea, to being the Queen of England and not having to wash the dishes, have been a few dreams I remember the children sharing with me. Thousands more were not.

As I turn on my right side to be more comfortable, I recognize favorite volumes of books in the bookcase that fits under the slope of the ceiling on the west wall. With our children and lots of neighborhood children that came over to play, the books have been taken off the shelf and read and re-read numerous times.

Curiosity finally pulls me upright in the bed. I still can't see the book spines well enough from here, so I get up and pull a small chair in front of the bookcase. One by one, I randomly pull out a book, thumb through the pages and put it back.

Läsebok för Småskolan, (*Reading Book for the Junior School*), published in 1885. "Hilda Olson, Star School" is written on the inside front cover. Mabel and Hilda must have switched books sometime in their playing. Hilda is Peter and Hannah's youngest daughter and Mabel's best friend. True opposites in nature, they have always had a close bond. Folded inside is a letter from Mabel to Hilda, asking her to come over and play. They used to love to write letters to each other and have their papas be the messengers whenever they would happen to come over or pass one of the farms.

Thin, easy reading books that tell a sweet story are signed to the children from their Sunday School teachers for Christmas gifts. The stories get longer and harder to read as the child advanced in class.

The copy of *Nya Testamentet och Psaltaren* (*The New Testament and the Psalms*) was used during confirmation class. I think that everyone studied harder for the oral examination of confirmation than all their school lessons combined. You could be forgiven by the school teacher and rework a lesson, but it was a different story with the pastor and confirmation. The children are tested in front of the pastor, the congregation and God. And they had to have it memorized and be ready. You never saw so many youngsters sweat in church as confirmation day.

Prärieblomman—Kalender för 1903. (*Prairie Flowers—Calendar for 1903.*) The book falls open where a flower has been tucked between pages to dry. I guess that's appropriate. Each year the Lutheran Augustana Book Concern has published an annual book of short stories and poems featuring people, places and topics of interest to the Swedish-American population. This edition has an article written by Dr. Carl Swensson. He wrote of how Dr. Olof Olsson came to the Lindsborg area, started the Bethany Church congregation, Bethany College and the annual performance of the *Messiah*. Birger Sandzen also has an article in it about Bethany College's art department. I enjoy reading articles about men I knew.

Dr. Swensson's life and career was cut short when he died of pneumonia in '04. Since he was only 46 years old at the time of his death, I wonder what other great things the man would have done in his later years. One never knows what is in store for a person's life.

Besides Swedish books, the children have learned to read English. Mark Twain's *Tom Sawyer*, first published in 1876 was a Christmas gift. I believe Alma sent Willie Twain's book, *The Tragedy of Pudd'nhead Wilson* when he was in California. Robert Louis Stevenson's *Treasure Island* rests on the shelf along with *Little Women* by Louisa May Alcott. It was a favorite of the girls and shunned by the boys because of the title. I'll let the grandchildren pick out a favorite book for them to keep.

I look up to see an old calendar tacked to the closet door. We left it up because it was a pretty picture. The only closet upstairs, it is used to store winter coats and clothing. When the seasons change, the articles in the closet do also. I'll have to remember to empty it, or we'll wonder where our coats are come October's first chill.

I still need to go through the dresser. I haven't peeked in the drawers for ages. When the children were living here, I'd occasionally glimpse special items hidden in their bureau drawers when I put away laundered clothing. I've been tempted to take a closer peek, but knew they needed their privacy.

The dresser drawers still contain a small variety of items belonging to the children. After Julia moved out of this room, I put the children's things in this dresser as I found them around the house. Although not full by any means, it seems like there are a few items from everyone. Some items that were so important in their lives were forgotten and left behind. They served their purpose during their growing up years.

Stashed in a cigar box are a variety of mementos. From the contents I'd say they belonged to one of the boys. A cat's-eye glass

54

marble, old stamps and half a chicken's wishbone are a few things that catch my eye when I shake the box. Calling cards collected from friends. A folded up program from a concert at Bethany College. Aha, the men's jewelry stick pin with the initial "W" gives away the identity of the owner of the box. Which girlfriend gave him that pin? I don't remember now.

Christine's autograph book with sayings from all her school friends is here in the bottom drawer. At age 25, will her daughter, Anna, want it for sentimental reasons if Christine does not?

I know, they are just like me. As I'm going through boxes, I'm thinking, "Why did I keep this?" It just took up space and added to the clutter. Other things, like the letters from Sweden, I wish I had kept. Why are certain things so important now? Because it triggers a special memory.

I wonder if any of the children, or grandchildren would like the contents of the dresser? I'm sorting them by child, if I can identify the owner. They can go through their boxes on Thursday. All their stuff is not going to be moved into Salina!

Here are some newspapers I had saved about the 1903 floods. That was during the rainstorms and summer flood that lasted about a month and seemed determined to sweep our farm down the river.

May 26th, 1903. One article's headlines read: *"Damage is Great—Hail Played Havoc with Skylights—Iron Roofs Punctured."* The other article says: *"Another Tornado—Wm. Olson Killed at Assaria Thursday."* Ben Olson's son was visiting his uncle's farm one mile east of Assaria when the tornado hit. William was killed and other members of the family were injured. The whole community mourned the loss of the child and pitched in to help clean up the destroyed farm.

The June 2nd issue's headline is: *"1000 drowned in Kansas City—The Missouri is higher than ever was known before and the destruction is frightful. The police given orders to shoot thieves."* That was a bad summer for all of Kansas.

Getting down to the newspaper lining the bottom of the drawers, I realize it's dated Match 5, 1912. I must have relined the drawers the spring after Julia was married. Looking at the articles makes me recall events that happened seven years ago.

"Seattle, Wash. March, 1—Two thousand young cherry trees, consigned to Mrs. Taft, at Washington, D. C., formed part of the cargo of the steamship, Awa Marn, which arrived here from the orient. The trees are a gift of the agriculture college of the Tokyo University."

"The News at Hallville" column listed our local news of who visited whom that week. Our family was mentioned. *"Joe Olson's visited at the Shogren home near Smolan Thursday and Friday."*

And here at the bottom of the column was the notice that my brother, Andrew had died. I thought I had cut that clipping out and saved it. I'll do that now while I think of it.

I pull the yellowed paper out of the top drawer. A small piece of cardboard flips through the air and lands at my feet. It must have been stuck up against the inside of the drawer and was dislodged when I took the newspaper out. It is a picture of a young man that one of the girls pined for after he left her. I know she has gotten over him, since she married another; but I'm naturally curious if she ever wondered how her life would have been if she had married him. We all question if life would be different if events didn't happen and change the course of our destiny.

Standing on the upstairs landing I can look back into the middle and north rooms. Boxes and trunks are stacked in the middle of the rooms. The bedding is stripped and the mattresses lay bare. Harsh extra light shines in the rooms since I took down the curtains.

My subconscious mind asks, "If I put everything back in its place, can we stay?"

Pausing at the top of the stairs, I think of all the trips up and down the narrow steps I've made. Over the years my pace has changed from quick light steps to slow ones.

These steps have made a variety of noises over the years: little ones crawling up the steps on all fours for the first time; stomping up mad after a fight and being sent up to their room; lightly pressed steps on the balls of their feet, trying to come in unnoticed at a too late hour (It never worked.); once or twice tumbling down when they tripped over a long hem or hidden toy on a step.

Grand descents by brides have been made from the top of these stairs. While little children who were relegated to stay upstairs for

56

the ceremony watched on, Carrie, Alma, Marie and Julia walked out of their childhood and into married life.

The wind blows just right around the corner of the roof and the shifting of the boards makes the attic door squeak. A person doesn't pay much attention to it during the day, but at night its another story. Will the wind scare the next child that spends his first night here sleeping upstairs? When I'm gone, will my ghost come back to this house to check on the sleeping children to make sure they are all right during the night?

It is awkward to open the trap door that opens from the south porch floor. There is very little space to stand to the side when you swing it open. Over the years I've learned to open it part way, then step down on the second step, then lean the door back against the west porch wall. Picking up the lit lantern, I make my way down the rest of the stairs that lead to the cellar entrance. I prop open the door and hang the lantern on the hook in the middle of the room. Making my way around the table in the middle of the room, I go up the north steps and push open the trap door that arises in the kitchen. With both doors open, it adds a little more light down here.

The cellar is under the dining room, the first part of our house. Sandstone rocks were laid one at a time after we dug the hole. That was so much work. I think I was the one that decided that 16 foot square was big enough for our first house, because I was tired of digging! After we got the wooden floor of the house in place so the cellar was covered, we moved some of our things from the dugout to the cellar until the house was ready for us to move in.

Separate from the storage room, is a narrow space directly under part of the parlor specifically designed as a storm cellar. Railroad ties stand on end to form an A-shape protection so the house won't cave in on us if we were down below when a storm hit the farm. The bottom of the ties are butted up against the base of the rock walls and the tops of the ties are bolted together. I don't store anything here during the summer because we wouldn't have time to clean it out and crawl in before a storm hit.

We've used the storm shelter more than once over the years. After one frightful experience with a tornado in '76, we never took the chance of staying above ground again when the weather was threatening. When helping neighboring tornado victims clean up after that storm, we saw how the house could collapse into the cellar if the wind was just right. When we built onto the east side of the house, we added this fortified shelter underneath the new addition for better protection.

Disasters have hit the cellar itself during a few floods, causing the water table to rise enough that there has been water in the cellar. The first time it happened I went down the stairs to get something for a meal and stepped in water. We had spent all our time making sure things were secure and out of water's reach in the outbuildings because of the rising water, never realizing there would be floating jars below us. All the food in the crocks had to be thrown out. At least there wasn't much new food preserved and stored since it happened at the beginning of the summer.

During the '03 flood we brought up everything we could. That was the flood that surged past the well and the house. Water poured through the crawl space holes in the foundation as fast as it could move. It took quite a while to bail the water, snakes and fish out after the flood and water table receded. It took months to finally dry out enough we didn't bring mud up on our shoes.

I'll have to inform the next woman who lives in this house what to expect when she sees the creek water rising toward the farm.

No matter where I live or how old I am, I'll always remember the distinct earthy smell of the cellar. Even without looking, I know what this room holds, and has held in the past because of the smells that permeate from the stone walls. Musty mold from the damp rock mixes with the smell of beef, potatoes, soap, candles, sulphured apples and pickles.

During the summer and fall we harvested and preserved the food we grew and stored it down here. Slowly over the winter and spring months we deplete our stock and start the process over as summer arrives.

Plain wooden shelves line the walls. Shorter shelves at the top of the wall hold pint jars of jellies and jams, and graduate to taller shelves that hold the heavy gallon jars of canned meat. Five and ten-gallon crocks with plates on top hold food that needs to be kept under brine, like pickled cucumbers. Other big crocks are used to cure and store meats after fall butchering. These sit on the floor, as do bins for potatoes, carrots and other root crops. My supply of soap bars is nestled in a box of straw. Although we don't use them very often since we have kerosene lamps, I continue to store the box of candles down here. They would melt if stored upstairs.

After fall butchering, slabs of fresh meat, rubbed with salt and spices rest on the room's table to cure before being cut up. It is then stored in barrels of brine, or smoked, wrapped in cloth and hung from the ceiling.

I was so thrilled when Carl brought home my first dozen jars from the general store. He had traded them for the butter I had made. Over the years the first twelve grew to hundreds. As each daughter left home to start her own household, I gave her a starter supply of jars. There was one less person to feed, so I didn't need as much food stocked for the winter.

All these jars will have to be carried upstairs for the move. Fortunately for the people carting them up these steps and down into the other house, half of them are empty. If it was late October, almost every jar would be full.

We have canned everything we could this summer so there will be a supply for winter. I reached through the thorny thicket for sand plums along the creek, plucked clusters of wild grapes from the vines, and picked individual purple currants from the bushes for the last jellies I'll make from the native fruits of this land. Mabel and I canned fruit as they turned ripe in the orchard and vegetables from the garden.

I close my eyes, point toward a shelf and recite:

Plum butter, currant jelly, cherry preserves, rhubarb marmalade. Pickled pears, watermelon pickles, sweet apple pickles, green tomato pickles, dill pickles. Canned corn, green beans, vegetable soup, beet relish, tomato juice. Pickled eggs, pickled pig's feet, canned suet, canned beef. . . .

No matter which way I turn, I know what and about how many full jars are on the shelves.

There is nothing more satisfying to a woman than to see her shelves full of stocked jars and know she has food for the rest of the year.

Although it doesn't pay to be smug. One year I boasted I packed a record number of jars on a shelf. Not too long after that we heard a mighty crash below the house. My worst fear had happened. The top shelf broke from the weight of the jars and crashed down the wall, taking all the shelves below it down also. It was a pile of glass shards, cracked boards and oozing fruit and vegetables.

I sat on the bottom cellar step and wept. We didn't have any cling peaches that year because every jar I canned that summer was in that section.

It was a headache to clean up. We couldn't feed it to the pigs or chickens because of the glass. What we ended up doing was scooping the syrupy mess into wash tubs and hauling it outside. Peter dug a big hole and buried the entire mess. If anyone ever digs very deep in the north end of the south field, they are going to be in for a surprise!

Wednesday, July 23rd

Greased with butter and lined up across the table in front of me are the six loaf pans that fit in my oven. Yesterday noon I cooked extra potatoes for the yeast starter. After dinner I mashed them fine and mixed with a little salt, sugar, flour, water and a yeast cake. Set aside and left alone, the mixture fermented all afternoon. Last night after supper, I added cooled scalded milk and cold water, then kneaded in warm flour to make a stiff dough. I returned it to the mixing bowls and covered it for the night. This morning I'm kneading the dough down to be divided into individual loaves for the pans.

I've baked bread every Wednesday and Saturday for over 50 years. Years ago I baked two batches twice a week. After the children left, I didn't bake nearly as many unless company or the threshing crew was coming. I'm baking the full oven load again today because of the help we'll have here the rest of the week for the sale and move. We'll be handing out sandwiches right and left to hungry people the next three days.

I had both the kitchen and utility room stoves stoked and going before the rooster crowed this morning. The rolling pin clanged and bumped out eight pie crusts first thing. Instead of lard, I used blocks of suet that I still had in the cellar. It makes excellent pie crusts. I draped the thin crust over the lined-up pie tins and Mabel went down the row, scooping canned fruit filling into each one. Two apple, two peach, one mulberry, one grape and two cherry. That got rid of a few more jars from the cellar. A dot of butter into each pan and another round of crusts on top. Pinching the two crusts together I sealed the edges against the rim of the tins. Slits to let the steam rise out of the crust during baking are appropriately cut to tell what kind of pie each is. "A" for the apple, "P" for peach, and so on. After pouring a little milk on top and sprinkling some sugar on each, they were ready to bake.

The loaves of bread are growing too rapidly underneath the towels that are draped across the floured tops. During the summer they rise so fast in the heat. During the winter, when the house is chilly, you wonder if the loaves will ever rise enough to bake.

The loaves need to get in the oven, but the pies aren't done yet. I can tell from the smell of the crusts when they are at the right tint of brown, and they aren't at that stage yet!

Trying to keep my patience with the stove, I go through my recipes looking for a certain one. What would I do without this old book. I started hand writing recipes in a school composition book years ago. Over the years I've collected recipes from friends and family and included them in the book. Most measurements are done by handfuls, or by "butter the size of an egg," but I know what they mean. They aren't in any order, so I have to hunt for each one, although I usually know whether my favorites are toward the front or back of the book. All the corners of the pages are worn from being turned so often. You can tell favorite recipes because the page is dirty from being open and splattered on by ingredients. Aha, here it is. . . Alma's Delicate White Cake. Light as a feather and topped with boiled icing.

My senses switch gears as i react to the smell coming from the kitchen stove. I think the mulberry pie has just oozed juice over the crust top and onto the bottom of the oven. I didn't need that today! The pies are coming out now, ready or not.

We move the pies onto the dining room table to cool and stick the loaf pans in the kitchen oven for their hour of baking.

That leaves the other oven available for cakes. I had thought about making an angel food cake today, but it needs to start with a cold oven, and I don't have time to let the oven cool and start over again. Angel food cakes take eleven egg whites, which leaves you with eleven egg yolks that I usually use in a sunshine cake. Today I'll make Alma's white cake that uses seven egg whites. The leftover yolks will be used to make mayonnaise dressing for the sandwiches.

Cinnamon, allspice, cardamom, thyme. . . A variety of smells penetrate the air when I pull my box of spice tins and extract bottles from the top shelf in my work cupboard. Even though the lids fit tight on the tins, little grains of spice get spilled in the box and give off an aroma. I should have left this box out because I have already pulled it out once today for cinnamon for the apple pies. Now I need vanilla for the white cake.

Holding the mixing bowl at an angle, I beat the butter and sugar with a wooden spoon until it is smooth and creamy. A teacup of sweet milk, then egg whites and extract are added next. Last added is the flour in which the baking powder had been mixed. Most recipes use the basic ingredients produced on the farm—milk, cream, butter, eggs and flour milled from wheat. These ingredients make everything from milk gravy on bread for breakfast, to cream puffs for supper's dessert. It will be different to go buy all these ingredients at a town store instead of milking the cow and gathering the eggs myself.

Thud! Thud! I drop each cake pan about three inches from the table's surface to knock the air bubbles out. Sure enough, several bubbles rose to the top of each. If I forgot this step, there would be big holes inside when the cake was cut. A true sign of a bad baker.

As I shut the oven door after shoving the cake pans in, Peter carries in two freshly plucked chickens that I asked him to get for me. With one hand I take the chickens, and with the other, I hand him the potato bucket which is empty. He grumbles under his breath that he has other things to do today as he ambles off to the garden to dig potatoes for dinner.

Lighting a cone of newspaper on fire outside the house over the washtub, I singe the pin feathers off the birds. Some women do this over the stove burner, but this fills the room with the putrid smell of burning feathers and I prefer to do it outside. I toss a dipper of water into the washtub to make sure the paper fire is out before I carry the birds inside. Expertly cleaning out the innards and cutting up the chickens, I put the pieces in a big pot of water on the back of the stove to boil until the meat falls off the bone. After fishing out the heart, liver and gizzard, I add them to the pot; then step outside and throw the innards into the cat's food pan. The two bravest felines pounce onto the pan to get the choice pieces and run off to savor their feast. The others are left to lick the pan and just get a taste of what they missed.

The cooked chicken will be put through the meat grinder after it has cooled. The broth will be boiled down to a thick liquid, mixed with the chicken and put in a mold dish. Lowered down in a bucket to the cool depths of the well, it will gel in the mold. By mid-afternoon, the pressed chicken will have set and can be sliced for afternoon lunch sandwiches.

The back porch door creaks open, a full bucket of potatoes hits the floor boards and then the spring on the door slams it shut. Mabel's about to pull the loaves of bread out of the oven, so Peter should just as well have stayed in for forenoon coffee. Rather than be occupied by ill temper, I must remember we both have a lot to do today.

Mabel heard the door too and retrieves the bucket. She'll wash and peel them for dinner's boiled potatoes and supper's potato salad. On my third trip to the cellar this morning I brought up a crock that had only two pickled tongues left in the bottom. The tongues are soon flapping in the boiling pot on the stove. Cooked, sliced and smothered in ketchup, they'll make good sandwiches for dinner.

Peter comes in the back door again, hangs his hat and washes up for coffee. I can't believe it's already 10 o'clock. Picking up a nearby knife, Peter cuts a big slab off a hot loaf. Dipping the same knife into the butter crock that I've had out to use for baking, he slathers the butter on thick and takes a bite as the butter melts into the bread. He still has the knife in his hand as he wanders into the dining room, eyeing the pies cooling on the table. I pour three cups of coffee and follow him, saying, "Those are for tomorrow!"

Mabel brings in a tin of rolled oatmeal cookies to appease his appetite. I've had a pinch of this and a pinch of that all morning while baking so I'm not hungry like he is. Men and growing boys have such appetites.

W. C. Curphey, the auctioneer who is calling the sale tomorrow, will soon be here to go through the machinery. I imagine he will have a young lad or two along to help move things around. Do I have enough planned for dinner? Besides tongue sandwiches, we can hard boil some eggs. Chopped up and mixed with mayonnaise dressing, egg sandwiches are filling. Extra boiled eggs can be made into deviled eggs for supper. Boiled potatoes, green beans cooked with a little salt pork for flavor, pickled beets, and a pie for dessert will complete the meal.

The auctioneer came with four extra men at mealtime. Besides the food we fixed for dinner, part of what we were preparing for supper was also eaten, besides two pies. I wonder if they will be here for supper too?

Mabel pours hot water into the pan of dirty dishes sitting in the sink in the corner where the north and west walls meet. We added this sink when we added the cistern and gutter system onto the house to catch rain water. A pitcher pump next to the sink brings water up from the cistern. We also installed a drain pipe that takes the water outside. I can catch the water at the end of the pipe if I want to save the water for flowers, or else it goes down a drainage ditch that runs north of the house out to the garden.

The base of the sink is enclosed with wainscoting painted white. It matches the kitchen walls that have wainscoting covering the bottom three feet of the walls, with a chair railing running along the top edge. The plastered walls above it are papered.

I reach for the tea towel that hangs from the wooden towel rack between the window and west door. Mabel chatters away about our visitors as she washes the dinner dishes. I dip them in the rinse pan, then wipe the surfaces with the towel. I've opened the big doors on the cupboard so I can put things away.

This cupboard on the south wall was built with wainscoting that was left over when we added it to the walls. It was a big improvement over the row of open shelves I had before. Built up to within six inches of the ceiling, the upper section has two 18-inch deep shelves, plus the waist-level base to put things on. The bottom half opens up to one 24-inch deep shelf. We didn't put a bottom shelf in, so things just sit on the floor inside the cupboard. With the cupboard being seven feet long, I have plenty of storage space.

Along with my dishes, cups and glasses, the shelves hold serving and mixing bowls, glass pitchers—everything a kitchen needs to prepare and serve food. The things I use the most are on the middle shelf. Wooden trays that I can lift out sit on the waist-high shelf. They contain everything from the silverware to wooden spatulas, cookie cutters, eggs beaters and other kitchen gadgets. The cherry pitter, apple peeler and sieve for pressing pulp are on the top shelf. I need a chair to climb up to get anything down, so it holds things that aren't used very often. Baking and cooking pans are stored in the shelves below.

Wiping the stirring spoon, I see the left side is worn down to a straight line instead of curved like a normal spoon. I have always used this spoon to stir gravy. You can tell I'm right-handed and have made many skillets of gravy over the years.

I still have two big wooden spoons that Carl carved for me. Yesterday I used the potato masher when I mashed the potatoes for the yeast starter. Most of my first utensils were handmade. They are now very dark with age and stains. Several smaller spoons have cracked and broken over the years and had to be tossed. The two-foot long wooden oval bowl Carl whittled out of half of a log is still used, along with a wooden paddle, to work out the buttermilk and mix the salt into the new butter after it is churned. I even used wooden butter molds before we had small crocks for that purpose. I remember on one lid he carved the petals of a flower, so that when it was pressed into the fresh butter, the block had that pattern on top. It is still on the top shelf of this cupboard.

I still use the sugar bowl he carved too. A squatish-looking bowl about eight inches in diameter, it has a lid that fits in the center. I'd say it roughly holds two cups of sugar. It has been on the kitchen table every day since it was made.

The pan I'm wiping now will soon be used again so I place it on the side of the stove over the water reservoir.

My big wood stove sits on the east wall to the left of our bedroom door and to the right of the north window. It has six burners, an oven, a warming oven on top and a water reservoir on the side.

I know my stove about as good as my husband—maybe better. I know how many pieces of kindling it takes to start a cold oven versus one where there is still some red ashes remaining; how hot the oven is and when I can start baking by how long I can stand holding my hand inside the opened door; how many minutes to heat a gallon pot of egg coffee to boil; and if the wind is coming out of the northeast during the winter, there is a chance I'll get a back draft and problems. I'll have to learn all the quirks of the stove in the new house next.

Split wood logs are added to the burner on the left side of the oven. I have a small wood box sitting next to the oven. During the winter, we keep a box on the back porch too so we have dry wood close by. Depending on what I am baking, I prefer different wood for different recipes because wood burns fast and hot or slow and even depending on how dense the wood is.

I also burn certain types of wood when I need ash. To prepare *lutfisk* for consumption, the dried boards of fish have to be soaked for days in rain water with sal soda and lime. Sal soda is made from burning hedge wood, so I always use that wood for a few days the first of December to get an ample supply.

I shove the clean measuring cup back into the right corner of the work cupboard table. This small cupboard to the right of the sink is my storage space for staples. The flour bin on the left side above the work surface holds about twenty-five pounds of flour. It fills at the top and funnels down to an opening in the bottom. Turning a little handle, the flour is sifted as it comes out of the funnel. Hanging to the right of the flour bin is the upside down glass jar of sugar. Moving a little side bar pushes a round circle of metal aside that covers the opening. Sugar falls into your cup or container until you move back the bar. To the right of the flour and sugar are two small shelves. The higher shelf holds my spice box that I pull down to get things out of. The lower shelf contains tins of miscellaneous essentials—baking soda, salt, whole peppercorns and such. It also holds medicines and salves.

Below the work space is another shelf. Here I store bottles of vinegar and molasses, large tins of oil, oatmeal and cornmeal, and a few pans that don't fit in the south cupboard.

I do most of my mixing and preparation on the table in the middle of the room. Here I have space to spread out my pie dough or cut up a slab of bacon. We've even had some minor and major surgeries on this table, performed by a doctor, or by ourselves if there wasn't help available. It served meals to a growing, then shrinking family. When we added on the kitchen, we ate here for a while before adding on the bedrooms. When the table in the dining room overflows with family or company, the children eat here at the kitchen table.

Spreading the wet towel back on the rack to dry, I know today's heat will soon have it dry. It's almost two o'clock. The heat is almost unbearable in the kitchen today since we used both stoves.

I wander out to the outhouse to use the facility, then out to the well for water to replenish the bucket in the utility room. The men will be in for afternoon coffee before I know it.

Slowly lowering the bucket on the rope that is attached to the pulley, it goes down the middle of the well. I feel the rope slack a bit when it hits the water's surface, then grow heavy as the bucket fills with water. Pulling the bucket back up, I reach inside the opening to grab the handle and pull the bucket out of the well. After pouring the cool contents into the bucket I brought from the house, I place the bucket on the rope on the edge of the well. Leaning over the well, my eyes adjust to the dark hole and I can see the small crocks and buckets dangling on ropes around the perimeter of the well's edge. The ropes are hung on iron hooks that hang right below the wood frame of the well. Being right above the water's surface and below ground, this well and the cistern hole on the back porch, also serve as coolers for perishable items. During the winter months, I can keep food on the back porch. It is a different story during the summer. Food spoils very fast in the heat, especially if made with eggs or meat. Rarely do we have fresh beef or pork during the summer, only chicken that can be killed, cooked and eaten on the same day.

Butter will last several days in the well. The well cooled this morning's milk before we drank it for dinner. I used the separated cream right away this morning in my cooking, but it usually is kept down there too. The best butter is made if the cream sets a few days to ripen before churning. In another hour, I'll pull up the pressed chicken that I lowered earlier today.

Bees buzz around the orange flowers of the trumpet vine that clings to the west side of the house. Ants love the nectar of the blossoms. A steady stream of them run up and down the vines and back to their ant hill. With just a few shade trees around the house, the vine gets a lot of sun.

There is a stepping stone walk that runs from the side gate, along the west side of the house, to the north porch door. Along the inside of the fence is my herb garden. It is close to the back door so it is handy for me to come out and snip a herb for cooking or medicinal needs. Originally I had started my herb bed by the well, but moved it after we added the fence. Prairie balm, yarrow, boneset. . . I dug these out of the native prairie the first years we were here. All the neighbors traded root starts of whatever each of us had. Adelaide Robinson gave me the mint starts years ago. They spread by underground runners each spring, so I have to chop it down to nothing each fall, or it would take over the farm. I plan to move a few starts to a patch beside the back door of my new home.

I refill the water bucket then walk back out of the house, reaching for the old broom as I go. Sweeping the utility room and back porch can be done twice a day on a farm and you will still have a dirty floor by sunset. I sweep the porch stoop too, then head along the north side of the house for the front porch with my broom and a bucket of rinse water from the dishes.

The row of currants we dug up from the creek and planted along the house years ago still flourish. In early May the air is fragrant with the sweet scent of the yellow teardrop-shaped currant flowers. Over the next few weeks tiny green balls swell into plump purple berries about the size of a pea. Currants make the best jelly.

I have to swing out to pass the lilac bush on the corner of the house. Planted years ago, it has become a very handsome plant. Some years it has been so loaded with blossoms the branches have leaned over. There were a few years when late spring frosts nipped the buds before they developed. Then I had to wait a whole year to enjoy them. I believe the lilac is my favorite flower.

The east porch was the last addition to our house. This is what people first see of our home since it faces the road. Built in the 1890s, it has victorian gingerbread trim that was so popular during that period. The spindles are painted in shades of green and yellow to complement the cream color of the house. The wood trim around the outside of the windows is also green.

From the porch, the house can be entered by either of two entrances, one from different additions to the house. Fancy screen doors cover the doorways. Our bedroom door has a plain wooden door. The parlor has a glass window on the top half. Besides giving that room more light, it helps people distinguish which is the "company" door to knock on. After putting the bucket and broom down, I ease down into the glider swing and rock in it for a moment. I wish I had time to sit here all day, idly daydreaming and sipping lemonade. Such is not the case for this old woman today.

Pouring a little of the water on the floor, I swish the broom across the boards to wash the dust off the porch. I want them looking clean for tomorrow. This is one job I thoroughly enjoyed doing barefoot during hot summer days. *Why not do it again?* Sitting back down on the swing, I unlace my high top boots and roll off my hose. I put them on the swing seat so they don't get wet. Oh! It feels so good to be barefoot in the cool water.

Growing up in Sweden, we went barefoot in the summer and wore thick wool socks with carved wooden shoes during the winter. Our one pair of leather shoes we had would be carried to church and then put on before we entered the building. It was about the same situation at first for all the immigrants here too. Carl had learned the shoemaker trade so our children were not without shoes for church. But during the summer months they didn't want to wear them unless it was Sunday.

Thinking I'll pick up my shoes in a few minutes, I go barefoot around the house to the south porch. The hot, dry grass blades prick my feet, except where the cedar tree on the southeast corner casts a shadow on the lawn. The dark stone step leading up to the porch burns my left foot and I almost stumble against the screen before I get it open. After stepping up on the porch and setting the bucket down, I stick my left foot in the water to cool it down. Ah, much better!

Washing down the boards, I see the paint is starting to flake a bit where we walk the most. Countless layers of paint have been put on over the years. We used to make the paint for the kitchen and porches and I think it wore better than the store-bought kind we painted with the last time. To make paint, stick glue is melted in a pan on the stove with rain water in which yellow ocher is added to give it a nice brown color. It dries the same day you put it on. Rub the floor freely with boiled oil and the floor paint wore like iron.

I slide the oleander plant over a bit so I can sweep under it. A few pink petals from a faded blossom have fallen behind the pot. I originally bought this plant for the parlor, but it got too big after a few years. Rather than throw it out, it sits on the porch during the summer. When the fall frosts threaten to freeze the garden, it's time to move this tropical plant to the cellar. There it sits semi-dormant until spring. On nice days in the late winter, I prop open the trap door on the porch and pull the plant toward the door so it gets a little sunshine. It will move with us on Friday.

This is the last time I'll wash this porch, so I stop to study it a minute. It has changed over the years. Starting out as a simple open porch to shade the south side of our new house, it was later upgraded to include trim poles like the east porch, and then screened in to keep the flies out. Well, if I keep reminiscing and dawdling like this about every room, I'll never be ready for Friday. Carrying the bucket and broom through the house, I deposit them in their place on the back porch and get back to work in the kitchen. The men will soon be in for afternoon coffee.

Because of the company I won't just pull out a tin of cookies this afternoon. Pressed chicken sandwiches, cake and egg lemonade will be served instead.

"Hum." Eyebrows raised, Peter clears his throat and looks down at the floor. Good heavens, I forgot to put my shoes back on! Here I am leading the men into the dining room barefoot. Blush runs up my cheeks like a school girl caught kissing a boy. Excusing myself, I go through the parlor and retrieve my shoes and hose from the porch. I head for our bedroom door instead of re-entering through the parlor in front of them. That's something the men will joke about for a while—the old farmer's wife that still goes barefoot in this modern age.

I think this is a good time to retreat to our bedroom. I still need to sort through our dresser. The men will go outside after coffee and supper doesn't need to be started yet.

Folded clothing takes up three drawers of the dresser. My underclothing—corsets, undershirts, slips and white handkerchiefs fill the top drawer. The next one holds Peter's clothing. The third stores seasonal items, like woolen long underwear and heavy socks. We can pull out the drawers when we load the dresser onto the wagon, then put them back in place for the trip, since they are not very heavy and have nothing breakable in them.

The bottom drawer is another story. The weight of the contents causes it to sag as I pull it out. I need to put at least half the contents in another box, or the drawer bottom will fall out on the trip to town. My knees are going to give out leaning over the drawer for very long. Getting down on all fours, I sit up with my legs under me on the floor beside the drawer and sort the contents.

Several anniversary books about the area add several pounds to the drawer. The Assaria Church compiled a small book entitled, *Vid Fyrtioårsfesten* (*About the Fortieth Year Festival*), to commemorate their forty years as a congregation. I thumb through the pages and formal portraits of charter members of the congregation stiffly look back at me. A brief summary on Måns Peterson and Bengt Hessler describes how these two men were among the first in the area and how they helped develop the town and instigated the start of the church. The book has a photo of each pastor that has served the church and his life history. The Hallville Chapel even

New and Old Assaria Lutheran Church buildings

rated a section with pictures of our congregation, groups and the building, inside and out.

What amazes me the most is the photo of the old church and the new brick one that was built a few years ago, side by side. Look how modern it looks; and it is. Electricity lines were run from Gypsum to Assaria, just so the church could have electricity. It has a furnace, lights, basement with a kitchen, classrooms and a large room for socials.

Assaria has grown at a respectable pace over the years. Businesses declined in the '80s, but it still has a main street full of shops. A Methodist Church was built in the west part of town at the same time the new Lutheran Church was being built. A high school was added to the Assaria school system. All twelve grades will be moving into a new three-story brick building as soon as it is completed.

Minnes Album Svenska Lutherska Församlingen-Salemsborg, Kansas-1869-1909. (Remembrance Book of the Swedish Lutheran Congregation, Salemsborg, Kansas 1869-1909.) Salemsborg Church congregation also published a large volume for their fortieth anniversary. It details with stories

Salemsborg Lutheran Church

and pictures everything that has happened to the church. It has a huge active congregation today, even though its district shrunk as Assaria and Smolan split off to form their own congregations.

I pick up the old Swedish Bible that made the trip to America in our trunk. Reading the Bible in one's own home was defying the Swedish ministers years ago, but most people had one anyway. It was used extensively in the dugout and at Salemsborg Church until we could afford a larger one.

This Bible reminds me of our first *Julotta* in Salemsborg's dugout church. Be-ing very pregnant and traveling at night during the winter was probably not a smart idea, but nothing could keep us from being in the only church in the area for Christmas morning. The cold, muddy room was filled with homesick Swedes; all longing for the touch and sound of the famil-iar to ease their pain of being separated from their home-land.

Bethany Lutheran Church

Lindsborg en Svensk-Amerikansk Kulturbild från Mellerstakansas (*Lindsborg, Swedish-American Culture in Central Kansas*) written in '09 and *Lindsborg Efter Femtio År* (*Lindsborg After Fifty Years*), just published recently, commemorate the activities of Bethany Lutheran Church, the town of Lindsborg and Bethany College. All three have flourished and are known world-wide because of the yearly performances of the *Messiah*.

The box that Carl carved for our homestead papers. I haven't looked in it for years. A rectangle box about twelve by sixteen inches, it is four inches deep and made from cottonwood cut from the river bank. The lid fits into a groove carved around the top of the box. That way, it can't fall open like a trunk lid and spill the contents. To open the box, I place my thumb in the little depression on top and try to push the lid aside. Warped from age and humidity, it doesn't want to budge. Getting up off the floor, I look for something on top of the dresser to help move it. Using the shoe horn for leverage in the hole, I whack the horn with the palm of my hand. The jarring motion frees the stuck lid enough that I can stick my fingers in the small opening and open it all the way. Sitting on the bed, I spread the contents out before me. It contains papers, letters, a coin and an old book. The items document the very first years of our lives on the prairie. This box stored all our important papers and mementos. If there was ever a danger of a prairie fire sweeping near our homestead, this box was to be with us when we fled.

This is where I put my letters from Sweden! I apparently didn't keep all of them, but I'll bet the most important ones. The very first letters we received were from our parents wondering if we had arrived safely in Illinois. They knew we were heading to Jacksonville to work for a friend. By the time we got their letters, we were thinking of moving to Kansas. Mail took so long to travel between the continents, that it took several months for us to receive a letter in Kansas after we wrote saying we were leaving Illinois.

Without opening the envelope, I know which letter contained the news that my family was following us to America. The ink on the address is smeared from the tears I wept. I read that letter so many times, I memorized the first lines. "File a homestead claim in my name. We'll be coming to America within the next six months." I was so happy to hear my parents would be near me again. I didn't think how hard it was for an old couple, almost in their sixties, to pull up roots and start all over on the open prairie. But I can see now that they did it to be near their children. I would do the same thing myself.

Carl's large family arrived the following year. His parents farmed to the northeast of us. Most of Carl's siblings settled in our area. A few homesteaded in other states. Some of the family I have kept close contact with, others I haven't heard from in years.

I pick up the gold coin and examine the surface. The front features the head of an Indian princess. The reverse side reads "3 Dollars" and is surrounded by a wreath. This coin was issued between the 1850s and 1880s, but never became very popular.

The train engineer toots the engine's whistle as he passes the farm. I turn toward the window to see the black smoke puff above the engine as it strains to pull its load up the grade to Hallville.

The view from the windows. It changes every time a person glances out. Whether it is to see who is coming down the road, or to watch an approaching thunderhead or snowstorm, I've appreciated having them. In the dugout I really missed decent windows so I could keep an eye on our surroundings.

For just a second, a shadow blocks the sunlight that had been coming through the tiny pane of glass in our dugout. The blizzard had stopped and the sun was glaring off the ice-crusted snow drifts. An hour earlier, Carl had bundled up and headed out in the sub-zero morning to try to find us some food. Now that the storm was over, he hoped the wild animals would venture out and he could shoot a deer or turkey.

That wasn't a passing cloud that closed off the light beam. I'm standing by the stove at the end of the dugout with my back to the door. There it goes again. I hurry around the table and peer out the little window. It is too small to be of much good except to look straight out. Who or what is out there? Shall I unbolt the door and peek outside? I hate to be afraid, but I don't want to be attacked either.

I also don't want to lose the heat I've finally generated in the house. Before I got the stove going this morning, there was a layer of ice in the water bucket. Carl had to dig out the snow drift that banked against the door this morning and the cold seeped in worse than usual.

Putting Christina in our bed with the quilts over her, I move back to the door. With my walking stick in my clenched hand, aimed and ready to defend us, I swing the door open.

76

A very young Indian woman stands shivering outside the door. An old buffalo hide whips around her in the wind. Is she alone, or a decoy for the men while they steal the livestock? She starts to move forward, holding a bundle out in front of her. The thing in the thin blanket slightly squirms and gives a whimper of a newborn. Why are the two of them out in this weather unprotected? Where is her man?

I motion the woman inside because she is on the verge of collapsing. We can't converse because of the language barrier, but she senses I can help them. Before closing and barricading the door, I peer outside around the corner again to make sure she is alone. Taking the bundle from her, I lay the infant on the bed and unwrap the blanket. The infant is just a few hours old and very cold. The tiny little girl needs to be warmed up quickly or else she won't live.

I wish I had a big cooking stove like I had in Illinois. It had a top warming oven at eye level above the stove's hot surface, just big enough to put things in to keep warm, like a pie, incubating chicken eggs, or premature babies. Right now, my small stove is going full blast to keep the dugout warm and can't be used for that idea. Setting my biggest pot on the stove to warm up the metal, I line the pot with a towel. After it gathers heat, I'll take it off the stove and wrap the baby in the warm towel and lay her in the pot. I hope the woman doesn't think I'm going to cook her baby for dinner!

By now, Christina has crawled out from under her hiding place. Pulling the tattered hide off the woman's shoulders, I point to the bed to get her to lie down in the warm quilts Christina just abandoned. She is a dirty mess, but I can wash things later. She lays there watching me as I tend her baby. Dipping a rag in warm water, I bathe the baby to get its circulation going. Slowly her skin turns pink instead of the blue tone it had when it first came in the door. Clothing her in an oversized diaper and shirt of Christina's, I wrap the baby in the warmed towel. Once the woman is rested and warmed up, I'll put the baby in the bed beside the mother so she can nurse.

Carl came back with food, which I cooked for the four of us. He had followed her tracks in the snow from the river to our dugout and was worried about our safety, not knowing it was a young woman in need.

The Indian stayed with us for a few days while the two of them regained their strength. One morning after breakfast, she bundled up the baby, pressed this gold coin from her shoulder bag in my hand and walked out the door toward the river. We never saw them again.

We could have dearly used that money to buy supplies, but I wanted to keep the coin to remind me that kindness to strangers is always rewarded in some way. I put the coin in the box for safekeeping, just in case we needed the money for an emergency.

I open a small book of handwritten notes. The spine creaks as I turn to the first page.

"March 7, 1868. Ellsworth, Kansas—I want to keep a journal of our adventure into the American Plains so I will have an account of what our first years were like."

My first journal. I wrote in this book whenever I could. Not so much to tell of our "adventure," but more of our survival. I was a very naive 23-year-old when I wrote that first entry. We didn't know what we were getting into when we left established Illinois. But we soon found out. Fortunately, unlike the Indian woman without her husband, Carl and I were together on the prairie with supplies and a shelter.

I turn pages, reading entries here and there. I wrote of frustrations and discomfort, worry, and sometimes terror. Everyday chores that are so primitive now to our modern conveniences. By just reading an entry, I can instantly recall the event I wrote about, or a family member that is now departed.

I have over a dozen journals of various sizes tucked in my bottom dresser drawer. When we get moved into town, one of my goals is to go back and read each one to relive my years on the farm. What should I do with them after that? Would one of my grandchildren like to save these journals and read them to their children someday?

The three large documents were the reason Carl made this box in the first place. Carl's handwriting at the bottom of this first sheet indicates this is the homestead application he signed at the land agent's office when we arrived in Salina the spring of 1868.

And here is my signature on the paper I filed after I had proved up the land in 1877. I went into Salina the winter after Carl was killed to get the land changed into my name. I was afraid that I might lose the land since it had been in Carl's name originally. I didn't want a claim jumper to take the land away from me after we worked so hard to clear the prairie.

The Homestead Certificate granting me the full legal title to the land. I remember a bittersweet feeling when I put this third piece of paper in the box. We worked so hard to homestead the land. But Carl never got the chance to see it proved up.

I look up and catch a glimpse of myself in the dresser mirror. Going back through these papers, I had slipped back in time and was young again. I stare at the lined face I see in the mirror's reflection. When did I grow so old looking?

THE UNITED STATES OF AMERICA.
To all to whom these Presents shall come, Greeting:

Homestead Certificate No. _285_
APPLICATION _13039_

Whereas, There has been deposited in the General Land Office of the United States, a CERTIFICATE of the REGISTER OF THE LAND OFFICE at _Salina Kansas_, whereby it appears that pursuant to the Act of Congress approved 20th May, 1862. "To secure Homesteads to actual Settlers on the Public domain," and the acts supplemental thereto, the claim of _Mary C. Swenson_, has been established and duly consummated in conformity to law for the _West Half of the North East Quarter of Section Thirty in Township Sixteen South, of Range Five West, in the District of Lands subject to Sale at Salina Kansas, Containing Eighty Acres._

according to the Official Plat of the survey of the said Land returned to the GENERAL LAND OFFICE by the Surveyor General.

Now Know Ye, That there is therefore granted by the UNITED STATES unto the said _Mary C. Swenson_ the tract of Land above described: TO HAVE AND TO HOLD, the said tract of Land, with the appurtenances thereof, unto the said _Mary C. Swenson_ and to _her_ heirs and assigns forever.

In Testimony Whereof, I, _Rutherford B. Hayes_, President of the United States of America, have caused these Letters to be made Patent, and the Seal of the General Land Office to be hereunto affixed Given under my hand, at the CITY OF WASHINGTON, the _27_ day of _December_, in the year of our Lord one thousand eight hundred and _Seventy Seven_, and of the INDEPENDENCE OF THE UNITED STATES the _One hundred and second_.

By the President: _R. B. Hayes._

By _B. S. Long_, Sec'y

S. W. Clark, Recorder of the General Land Office

Recorded, Vol. _6_, Page _423_,

STATE OF KANSAS, _Saline_ COUNTY, ss.

THIS instrument filed for record this _19_ day of _Decbr_ 188_2_ at _2_ o'clock _P._ M., and recorded. _A. Ackmann_ Register of Deeds.

The Homestead Certificate

In the bottom of the box is a piece of paper that was folded like an envelope. I carefully unfold the yellowed sheet to uncover a locket of Carl's blonde hair. It will forever be a young man's hair. He would have been 80 years old this year. What would he have looked like as an old man?

Thursday, July 24th

I couldn't sleep. The words "We're leaving the farm, we're leaving the farm," just kept echoing in my head as I tossed and turned in the damp sheets soaked with my sweat. Peter was exhausted from yesterday's work and snored away. I finally got out of bed and slipped out the bedroom screen door to the porch. Leaning against a porch post, I stare into the night.

Most of yesterday evening's clouds had passed through the sky leaving a night brilliant with millions of stars. Searching the heavens, I find several constellations I recognize, like the Big and Little Dippers.

I helped the children learn to find them. First it was Christina that Carl lifted up on his shoulders so she was above the tall grass. Next Willie. With the younger children, we spread blankets on the lawn and laid on the ground. Their little head was in between ours so our line of vision was the same. Pointing an arm to the sky, they could follow our finger to what we were seeing. Oh the excitement when they finally grasped the outline of the Big Dipper. Squeals of delight, then silent ahs of splendor. Their universe had just expanded beyond the earth.

The Kansas sky. It seems so different than the Swedish sky I remember. Because we were closer to the Arctic Circle in Sweden, we had summer daylight that lasted past midnight. Winters were the opposite with much more night than day. I think we had more cloudy days too, so we couldn't see the stars as often.

I remember searching the stars at night up on the ship's deck on our trip to America. I hated the feeling of not being in control of the ship. We were at the mercy of a crew that we didn't know. Would they get us to land, or would we circle the oceans forever? I looked for the North Star every night. That star was my beacon and my assurance that we were on the right track and had made the right decision. Are we making the right decision now?

The milking shorthorn cow looks at me like she's thinking, "What do you think you're doing?" It's been a while since I milked the cow. But this is my last opportunity, so she is going to be milked by me.

A manger of sweet hay changes her mind anyway, especially since she knows me. This cow better enjoy it too, because she'll be in a different barn and milked by strange hands tonight. Sitting the bucket under her, I hitch up my long skirt and balance my seat on the homemade milk stool that consists of a two-foot section of 4 by 4 post, with a square of lumber nailed on the top of it. I lean into the cow's side and reach into her warm udder for the teats. Getting the rhythm of the hand squeeze going, the streams of warm milk start to flow and froth in the bucket. The barn cats come out of the hay mow and stretch out a safe distance from the kick of the cow to wait for their breakfast. Taking a sideways aim with the teat, I squirt and miss the first cat, but the second shot is a bull's eye. The cats are going to have to find mice for supper tonight since the cow will be gone. They are wild and will stay with the place. Soon someone else will be milking a cow here and the cats will get back in the routine of waiting for their squirt of milk.

Once you learn how to milk a cow, you never forget. As a young girl, my summers were spent in the high pastures tending the cows. We didn't have a fenced place to go to. We just followed the cows around as they grazed on the grass in the rocky high land. The sound of the bell on the cow's collar kept us from ever losing them if they wandered into the wooded area where we couldn't see them.

We milked the cows out in the open. They were docile and didn't need to be tied up. Butter and cheese were made out of the surplus milk we got in the summer. During the cold, dark winter, the cows mostly stayed in the barn, content to sleep between milkings.

It is still half-dark outside when Peter walks into the barn. He got up to milk the cow, but the pail was missing from the utility room and he couldn't find me. He says out loud the same the cow was thinking earlier, "What do you think you're doing?" Even though I have tears in my eyes, I laugh and take aim with the teat at his shoes and make another bull's eye. For a little while, I'm a young milk maiden again.

This is the third barn we've built through the years. The first was a small crude shelter that we kept adding on to as we had money for lumber. It housed our first animals and stored the first grain crops off the fields. Eventually we dismantled it after we built the big barn in '93.

Runeberg's 1893 barn

Two stories tall and painted red, the second barn was a massive American-style building. The downstairs was partitioned with four individual stalls on the south side for the draft horses, with the end space being a lower manger and place to stand and milk two cows. The north side of the barn had two box stalls that could hold four saddle horses. These were also used for a cow with a newborn calf if they needed to be inside. Also on the north end was an enclosed tack room to hang the saddle and bridles, and a grain room for the supply of oats for the horses. The collars for each draft horse hung

83

on the post by their stall. The harnesses hung on the wall beside the tack room door. Movable doors on tracks opened up on both ends to bring animals in and out, as well as breezes for circulation during the summer. The staircase on the left as you came into the barn climbed up to a trap door that opened to the upstairs.

This barn was tall enough to have a huge haymow upstairs to store the whole summer's worth of hay. The top west end had a large door that slid open. The hay was lifted up by a big hay hook from the wagon below and hoisted inside the barn by a pulley system. A track ran the entire east to west length inside the barn so you could drop the hay wherever you wanted.

The racket and commotion caused by the dog barking on the west side of the house finally made me curious enough to check what he was barking about. The two of us just finished our supper and had gone out to sit on the front porch. Mabel had left earlier with friends.

It had been a scorching hot, unsettled day. A hot, unrelenting wind had blown all day and was just starting to die down a little with the sunset. Peter spent the day plowing the north field. Not one hour ago he had brought in the horses, took off their harnesses and fed them their evening ration of oats. While I washed the supper dishes, he turned the horses out of their stalls and into the corral for the night.

I heard a dull roar and cracking sound above the wind as I rounded the south corner of the house. I was watching my steps, but then my path was lit as a burst of orange flames explodes through the front upper story window of the barn. In reflex reaction, I threw up my arms up to shield my face and screamed as I staggered backward. After catching my balance, I ran toward the burning building. Peter heard the noise and was right behind me.

The barn is on fire! I've got to save what's inside!

Peter grabbed my arm and drug me to the water supply tank by the well. "Get water!" I grabbed a bucket by the tank and hastily skimmed a little water in the bucket and doused my head. My adrenalin jerked two buckets deep through the water this time. Heaving the heavy over-flowing buckets over the side of the tank, I staggered to the barn door.

84

Smoke rolled down the staircase and out the front door. It was impossible to enter this way. The cupola, or what's left of it, tumbled down from the roof in a ball of fire. The south wind picked up and tossed burning shingles into the air current. What if a spark lands on the granary roof?! We're losing our hay crop and one building. Will the summer's harvest of wheat be next?!

The horses were out in the corral, circling, screaming for their own safety. We went around the north side of the barn and Peter opened up the corral gate. As I chased the horses out of the corral, Peter shouldered the back barn door open. We each splashed a bucket's worth of water into the doorway to clear the air before entering, carrying the other bucket with us for safety. The tack room is on this end of the barn. Feeling his way along the wall, Peter reached high up to get the first harness off its horn hook. Throwing the 50 pound set of leather straps on my shoulder, he reached for the next one while I dragged it out the door. Grabbing two more sets himself, he half carried, half flung them out the door. I yanked the last set off the wall, bringing the horn with it. Reaching across the aisle, Peter pulled off two horse collars on the posts between the stalls, but dared not go to the front two stalls because the flames had spread down the steps and across the first two stall mangers that were full of hay. Feeling along the wall, I found and turned the block of wood that held the tack room door shut. Since the door was closed, the smoke had not penetrated this room yet, but it was starting to seep through the floor boards above me. The saddle, with its blanket thrown on top, sat on a horizontal board on the east side of the room. Pulling it down, I started to go out the door with it. Peter grabs it from me, threw it over his shoulder and heads both of us out the door.

Shouts from Joe and Julia were muffled in the sound of the fire. They must have seen the fire from their house and come over. Panic filled their voices because they couldn't find us. We had to get out before they tried to enter the burning building! Crouching low, we inched our way back out the way we came in. I heard a little meow. Was it coming from the nest of kittens in the cow's manger? I had forgotten about them. I tried to pull my hand out of Peter's grasp, but he wouldn't let go. Stumbling over something, I fell on one knee and caught myself with my right hand. A ball of fur! I stumbled onto the kitten! I grabbed the thing with my free hand as Peter pulled me out the door.

Wheezing from the smoke, we came around the corner to see a brigade of people, passing buckets, trying to put out the fire. Rushing up to us, two of them poured buckets of water on us. I hadn't noticed yet, but my skirt had burn holes smoldering all over, as did Peter's shirt.

Neighbors had seen the flames and came over to help. Someone had called the neighborhood on the general telephone party line, so people arrived as fast as they could with buckets, shovels and gunny sacks in tow.

We were so stupid to enter the building, but our reaction was to save what we could. We built our lives around this farm and couldn't bear to lose a part of it. But our children could have lost us instead.

Finally the men gave up on the barn and started throwing water on the granary roof.

I stood in silence, holding the kitten, watching the flames destroy my barn. An hour later, there was nothing left but the smoldering foundation.

That happened on Thursday, July 29, 1917. We lost the barn, but saved the rest of the buildings. We decided it was hay combustion from the fresh hot alfalfa in the haymow that started the fire.

That fall we built again on the old foundation, the same size and layout as the old barn. Since it is only two years old, the smell of new lumber and paint still greets us at the door along with the usual barnyard smells.

Before I finish milking, I give Smoky, the cat that survived the fire, one last squirt of milk. Then I give the cow a pat so she knows I'm moving. I get up and lift the milk bucket out from under her. Hanging the milk stool back in its place on the wall, I carry the bucket out the barn door.

I'm a little early gathering the eggs this morning, but I need to get back to the kitchen. The chicken house and pen sit a little distance to the northwest of the house, close to the granary. It has one door on the south, that is used to go in the building, and one

Chicken House

that enters into the pen. Inside the chickens have a sloped roost they sit on at night while sleeping. The nests are in rows of boxes attached to the outside of the building. The chickens go through a hole in the wall to get to the nests. To gather the eggs, we don't have to go into the chicken house, just lift the hinged top boards of the nest boxes.

I see most of the nests still have chickens laying eggs in them. I reach underneath the chickens and pull the still-warm eggs from underneath them. One old hen pecks at my hand, but I give her tail feathers a yank and she jumps through the opening back into the hen house. One of us will have to come back out later to get the rest of the eggs. The chickens crowd around the pen gate, waiting to be let out of the pen to spend their day scratching around the farm. That won't happen today. They will be sold during the sale, put in cages and hauled away squawking. Some will end up in another pen tonight, others a family's frying pan.

We usually set about 200 eggs each spring. The setting hens are moved to the brooder house on the south side of the house to set on the nests until the chicks hatched. A small mesh wire pen kept the chicks safe during the day. When big enough, they were moved to the chicken house. Most of the old hens went in the stew pot during the winter, so there was room in the chicken house for the new set of chickens. When they are big enough, they start laying eggs. When we had a surplus of eggs, we traded them for groceries in town. The store needs eggs for their town customers that don't have chickens.

The chickens are our main source of fresh meat during the summer. Depending on how many people we're feeding at a meal, one or several chickens may have their neck wrung by noon.

This spring, since we decided to move, I didn't set as many eggs. I wanted enough to last through the summer, but not have half a pen full left. I wish I could have a small pen of chickens in town. I'll miss gathering eggs.

Since the chickens can't come out, I'll give them a bucket of grain this morning. I think there is still a small sack of wheat left in the granary. The side shed doors have been pushed open on their tracks, letting light and breeze inside. There are four inside rooms; three used for bulk grain storage and one for sacks, tools and so on. The inside granary doors are high up on the walls. A team of horses would bring in a wagon load of grain and stop at an opening. The doors are just the right height so that you could scoop the grain inside the bin while standing in the wagon. The team could come in one door and pull out the other without having to back out. I know these bins have been cleaned out and the wheat hauled to the elevator, so I walk around back to the west room.

I stop in my tracks. I hadn't been back here for a day or so. Behind the granary, out of sight from the house, our machinery is lined up in rows, ready for the sale today. Of course I knew this was where Peter, the auctioneer and his helpers spent yesterday between meals, but I hadn't been out to see their progress.

It is like looking at the invention and progression of farm machinery. Implements have improved drastically over 50 years. I move to stand behind our first one-bottom plow and reverently put my hands on the handle. I took turns using this plow with Carl. Even though it was so much work to use, I loved it because the alternative was break the sod one shovel full at a time. Closing my eyes, I can feel the strain of the ox pulling it through the unbroken sod, the shaking of the plow as it is pulled below the surface of the grass.

Step by step, the ox strained against the wooden yoke. It was almost too much work for the single animal and I was pushing the plow from behind to help it along. I wish we had money to buy a second animal. It was taking forever to plow this small area. Both of us needed frequent breaks to get our strength back.

The thick strip of sod turned over to reveal warm, fragrant, black crumbly earth, teaming with earthworms and other underground life. A mouse was disturbed from its underground nest and scurried away to unturned ground. At this slow place you see and sense what is going on around you. A huge hawk was circling above us. What was he watching? The mouse headed the other direction. Swooping down to the left of us, the hawk dived for his prey and headed for the sky again with a snake writhing in his claws. I shuddered thinking we would have been plowing in that area soon. A snake bite could have killed either me or the ox.

Collecting my courage, I pushed the plow again. This work must be done to plant the crop or else we'll starve next winter.

This plow was replaced with a two-bottom plow, then a riding one that was pulled by a five-horse hitch. Sickles, cultivators, rakes, wagons—some ancient models, others fairly new. We started out with this one plow and now have three rows of machinery lined up.

The hay wagons have tools and miscellaneous items piled on them. The harnesses we risked our lives for in the barn fire hang on the back of one wagon. The auctioneer will stand on the wagon above the crowd and call for bids while his helper holds up the item that is selling at the moment.

I turn my back on the machinery and go back to the granary for the bucket of wheat I had originally come for. The west bin is empty except for two sacks of wheat and a pile of boxes in one corner. Stepping inside the room, I wait a minute for my eyes to adjust to the dim light. I fill the bucket, then put it down while I check the contents of this room. The corner holds a few tools that Peter will bring to town with him: two shovels, the hand rake, a pitch fork—

things to keep up the yard. A couple of wooden boxes hold saws, hammers, hand drill, screwdrivers—tools to make house repairs.

In the dark corner I also see the saddle blanket covering a large lump. I peek underneath to find the saddle hidden underneath. Why on earth is he keeping the saddle? We won't have a horse in town. He's just like me and being sentimental. We both want to keep something from the past. Tucking the blanket back under the saddle, I make my way back to the waiting chickens.

Goodness! Why did I bother baking pies and bread yesterday? A steady stream of friends have come in the back screen door into the kitchen, their arms laden with food. Every neighborhood woman brought two pies or cakes to serve for the food sale table and one of something for our family. My daughters and daughters-in law also brought baskets brimming with food for the day. I should have realized this always happens. I've done the same thing at other neighbor's sales. It is just one of those things us women folk do. It's our way of helping out a neighbor.

Big pots of coffee are simmering on the summer kitchen stove. Members of the Hallville Chapel are selling coffee and food as a money-making project at today's sale. Young people from the Luther League have set up a table on the west side of the house and will be going in and out of the house today. Mabel will oversee the project, so I don't have to worry about it. I know these young people and trust them all.

Looking out the open parlor door, I see wagons, buggies and a few automobiles lining up and down the road that runs beside our farm. Farmers are leading their teams to the water tank by the barn. After the horses have drank their fill, they will be tied in the shade of the barn to await their trip home.

People are walking by the house, some boldly coming through the yard gate and peeking in the windows as they pass. One stranger opened up the parlor door as if to walk through the house on the way to the farmyard. I stepped in his way and politely as possible asked if he needed directions to the machinery. It's eerie, almost as if I'm already gone from this farm and my ghost is watching the scene.

Runeberg House

Being close to the road, we've always had a large share of strangers stopping in for directions, shelter or food. The types of people have changed over the years. We fed the innocent pioneer families coming from the civilized East. Heading across the country the wrong time of year, we often wondered if they survived.

In the early years, very few salesman showed up at our door, because it was not worth the peddler's time to hunt for dugouts in the prairie floor. Later, you could count on several a week. Some were genuine, others frauds, but they sold everything from windmills to medicine out of the back of their wagon.

After the railroad came through our land, people who were hitching rides on the train, or walking the rails, would stop when they saw a water well so close to the track. Men walking by the farm are almost a daily sight during the summer. Most are polite, but I know a few have stolen eggs from the chicken house, or apples from the orchard.

Every now and then someone would come along that we would have to chase off with the gun. Cattle drivers with the longhorn cattle drives had a bad reputation, and some of it was justly earned. Horse thieves and cattle rustlers would sweep the county stealing livestock. Bands of roving gypsies would steal everything from chickens to dishes if you weren't careful.

From the west dining room window I can see people snooping around the buildings, opening doors that Peter had purposely shut for the day. The farm buildings aren't for sale, but people are curious.

The place does look nice. Peter trimmed the grass and weeds around the buildings and repaired a few things that have been neglected for years. He even used up some old paint on gates around the corrals.

Neighbors and family mill around the farmyard, talking to each other, greeting others as they walk down the driveway and join the group. Strangers, some gawkers, others looking like serious buyers, mill around the machinery. One man parked himself in our buggy. Either he intends to buy it, or just wants a place to sit. Women stand under the few shade trees around the house, fanning themselves and gossiping about neighborhood events. The temperature is starting to rise. I hope the church group has made enough iced lemonade for the day.

The auctioneer opens up his pocket watch, and shows it to Peter. As Mr. Curphey strolls toward the row of machinery, Peter walks toward the house. It is time to start the auction and he hasn't seen me outside yet.

I sniff back tears as the lump in my throat grows. How am I going to get through this day? The idea of a sale seemed like a good, and necessary thing at the time we set the date, but now I want to turn back the calendar.

"*Det är dags.*" "It's time," Peter says in Swedish as he comes up behind me where I stand at the window. Taking his hand, we go out to start the auction.

We stand together to welcome the crowd and thank them for attending our auction. Peter tells them we're looking forward to retired life in Salina, all the while squeezing my hand so hard it almost hurts.

The auctioneer climbs up on a wagon and raises the first item to bid on. People shift their gaze from us, to the pitchfork in the auctioneer's hand. A pitchfork changed my life once. It's only fitting the same tool would start the sale that is changing my life again. The sale has started. There is no turning back.

Someone asks Peter a question about the cultivator and he drops my hand to walk over with the man to that piece of machinery.

Most people are softly talking among themselves, only half listening to the auctioneer. Unless they are wanting to bid on something, they are just here to be at a social gathering, to see who was at the auction and what price items brought.

"Who bought that harness?," Minnie asks me. I don't know everyone at the sale. People outside our community have descended on the farm today. Implements and animals will be scattered among neighbors and strangers alike.

Children play around the farmyard, not paying any attention to the adult crowd. Individuals occasionally break away from the crowd to buy refreshments, get a drink of water from the well, or use the outhouse.

"Do I hear two bits? Yep! Now three. Yep! How about a dollar? A dollar? No? Well, going once, twice. Sold for seventy-five cents to the man in the back." As the smaller items are sold, they are passed to the person winning the bid. Slowly the items piled on the wagon dwindle down to nothing. People stand holding their items, not wanting to leave the bidding. Others carry them back to their wagons. A few people leave when they get, or miss what they came to buy. The day drags on.

As is tradition, the small things are sold first, saving the best for last to keep the crowd at the auction. I've watched some things sold. Other times, I've been asked questions and had my attention drawn away from the sale. After being in the house one time to check on the food sale, I went out the parlor door to the road, just to see how far the vehicles stretched.

When we first arrived on this land, there wasn't even a trace of trail in the tall grass. Over time, as we traveled to and from the Robinson's to the north and our families homesteads to the south, a little path formed, a part in the sea of grass. Other travelers found the path and soon it widened into a trail. Now it is a maintained township road, used every day.

The crowd has left the machinery and is slowly milling behind the auctioneer as he walks to the chicken house. Lifting my skirt, I clumsily climb over the low fence between the road and the farm. Cutting through the orchard, I hurry as fast as is decent toward them. I do want to see who gets our chickens. Sold in lots of a dozen at a time, the hens will scatter to area farms. Julia wanted the old bantam rooster, so it stayed locked up in the chicken house during the sale. Frustrated at not being able to be outside, it has paced the chicken house and crowed all day. Tonight the rooster will have a new roost to sit on in Julia's chicken house.

Now everyone heads for the barn, where the animals are waiting in their stalls. They are the last items to be sold on the farm.

The six pairs of cows and calves are sold from where they stand in their pen by the barn. At the moment they wonder why a crowd of people are staring at them. Their biggest surprise will be when they are cornered and driven off to another pen this evening.

Peter leads out the mooing milk cow who suspiciously eyes the crowd. Changing her mind about being the center of attention, she puts the skids to her feet, jerks the rope out of Peter's hand and returns to the barn. Moving out of the crowd, I step into the barn after her, calling her name. Softly singing to the cow, like I did this morning when I milked her; she calms down and lets me lead her back outside. People first thought we were trying to sell a spooked cow, but when I led her around in a circle they realized it was only the situation. She is following me like an old dog wanting attention. The bidding echoes around the cow and I. Unfortunately it doesn't last forever. Her lead rope is taken from my hand and she's led away.

Willie and Alfred lead out the Percheron draft horses, who have been tied in their barn stalls today. Serious buyers circle the team, coming up to run their hands down a leg and pull up a hoof to check the condition of the feet. A man opens up one of the horse's mouth to check her age by her teeth, as if Peter would lie about their ages. The mare of this pair of horses came from the Lamer Percheron Stud Farm near Bridgeport, so they are from high quality imported stock. The bidding ends at a respectable $350 for the pair. I know the neighbor that ended up with the pair will take good care of them. The horses are led back to their stalls until the farmer is ready to take them home.

Next the Morgan team, Maude and Jim, are led out and looked over. This pair of sorrels has taken us all over the county. Whether

Julia, Earland, Kajsa and Peter

it was taking the girls by buggy to a literary meeting in Assaria, me by wagon to get groceries in Bridgeport, or pulling the buckrake in the hay meadow, they have always worked as a pair since they were broke to pull. Since we purchased a touring car a few years ago, the team was mainly used around the farm. An older man who bought the surrey, also bought the horses.

That left the saddle horse to be sold. This chestnut gelding with the white blaze on his forehead was young when Peter bought Jack seven years ago. When I first saw him, I was afraid he was going to be a little feisty, but he quickly proved me wrong. Over time Jack mellowed out to be a very good horse, although he never got very big. Whenever the grandchildren came over to play, he patiently stood by the fence so the young ones could crawl up on the gate and onto his bare back. Sometimes there would be four or five kids piled on his back and he was still good-natured. Not all the horses we've had on this farm would let a child or grown-up do that. This horse has been special.

The crowd is thinning out. After this horse, the sale is over. People are starting to hitch up their teams to their wagons out on the road. Some will drive in to load up machinery or tools they bought. Some will come back for it this evening after they have delivered the family home in the wagon and done their own farm chores.

On and off all day I had been noticing a neighbor boy, Carl, who is about ten, slip into the barn from time to time. Checking in on him once, I saw he was not causing mischief, just quietly talking to Jack. Now as the auctioneer gets ready to start the bidding, the boy stands beside the horse, putting a hand under the horse's head to scratch his chin. The boy looks back at his father once, who gives him a nod of assurance. Then he turns back and stares intently at the caller. People sense the boy wishes he had the horse, but does he have money and plan to bid on it?

"Where should we start the bid?," asked the auctioneer.

"Ten dollars," said the boy, getting up his nerve to show he was serious about owning the horse.

A cocky young man about eighteen, who I didn't know, quickly upped the bid. I wasn't sure if he wanted to purchase the horse, or just see the lad suffer. Apparently Carl was serious about buying Jack, because he bid again. So did the young man. By now, I was silently rooting for Carl because I knew he would be perfect for the horse. I could see Peter thinking the same thing. There was another neighbor or two that had looked at the horse earlier in the week, but they sensed the boy needed the lesson, good or bad on how to buy a horse, and stayed out of the bidding.

Dollar by dollar, the two bidders inched up past twenty dollars, then forty. I knew the horse could bring up to seventy-five to a hundred dollars, but I didn't know if Carl had that much money. People who had been ready to leave stuck around just to see the outcome of this bidding war. Carl quickly counted his money and realized he was at his pocket limit. The older boy sneered and raised the bid another dollar.

"Going once, . . . going twice."

"Wait," Peter said to the auctioneer, holding up a dollar. "I believe the lad dropped this bill and would like to up the bid with it."

"Sold to the young lad!," barked the auctioneer before the other boy could think what to do.

Carl's jaw dropped. He had bought the horse. In time, I'm sure he'll realize that the dollar bill that helped buy the horse didn't drop from his pocket, but right now he was ecstatic. The crowd claps a round of approval and I beam at my husband. Jack was going to a good home and rider thanks to Peter's help.

The whole family is on the east porch discussing the day's event while we eat supper. There were so many leftovers in the kitchen that I didn't even bother to heat up the stove.

Children and grandchildren with Peter and Kajsa

"What price did the cultivator bring? Who bought the manure spreader? Did you taste that delicious raisin cream pie Millie brought?" I listen to the chatter. This sale didn't affect their lives as much as it did mine, although they all feel the loss of our moving off the homestead. But we all know that life changes and we must make the best of it.

I wish Alma could have been here today, but it was too far for her to travel. Of all the children, I think she was the most attached to the farm and animals. And as it turned out, she had to leave it, just like I'm about to.

The house is so quiet now that the children's families have gone home. The house literally vibrated with grandchildren running up and down the stairs and in and out screen doors. Talk and clanging of my pots and pans mixed together in the kitchen. With so many hands to help, we finished packing the house tonight. Just a few essentials in the kitchen and bedroom are left to pack in the morning. They'll be back tomorrow to move the last of the household furniture into town.

Sitting out on the porch in the glider swing again, I stare at the black sky. Stars twinkle above me again like they did early this morning before dawn.

I survived the day, but I am exhausted.

Friday, July 25th

Somewhere in the distance a meadowlark is singing. The bird's five-note song is drifting above the sea of green waving grass. Standing up in the wagon, with my hand over my eyes, I search for the direction of the call. I marvel at the rolling land that seems to be constantly moving, and almost expect our wagon to move in the waves like the boat that carried us to America. The baby-fine hair of Christina brushes my face as she turns her head from my shoulder to glance around. Although somewhat apprehensive about this untamed land, I look down and smile at the baby in my arms. My proud husband, Carl, sits in the wagon seat, surveying the land for which we just signed papers and on which we'll start our new life. He meets my eyes and flashes a reassuring look.

I hear the meadowlark again and realize it's a dream. This is my last day on the farm, not the first.

What I wouldn't give to close my eyes again and drift back fifty years. We were so young and strong. No matter the hard work or setbacks, we worked together and hand by hand, built this farm from scratch.

But now I reach out and feel Peter, still soundly asleep beside me. Carl and I started this homestead together, but Peter and I have worked side by side the past forty years. Peter stirs, searches for my hand lying beside his in the middle of the bed, and closes his hand on top of mine. Together we lay there, listening to our farm waking up as the sun slowly rises in the cool morning.

It seems so strange not to waken to the rooster crowing this morning before dawn. After pausing at the outhouse this morning, I automatically headed out to the chicken house to open the gate, but then realized the pen was silent. It will take me a while to unlearn the countless years of chore routine.

Egg gravy. It has always been our staple meal no matter how poor or rich we've been. No matter how low the staples were in the pantry or cellar, we always had eggs, milk and a little flour. It just seemed like the right breakfast to fix for our last meal on the farm. Even though the chickens and milk cow left yesterday, I still have their cherished produce to use this morning.

Joe's team methodically plods on at a slow pace, waiting for Peter to pull them to a stop once again. Since we sold our team and buggy yesterday, we're driving Joe's around the perimeter of the farm this morning for one last look at our land. Stopping often, pointing to a spot where something important or ordinary happened, we reminisce about the farm's past.

Just out of our driveway and heading north, we get the full view of a train heading east. The engineer waves at us. Since we are so used to it, half the time we don't even hear the chug of the engine

Train going past farm

unless we're outside and see it pass. This is about the only noise that breaks the stillness of the countryside. I fear we'll have trouble getting used to all the sounds of the city.

Earlier in the month the north field was a stand of golden wheat, the heads bent down, ready to be cut. Threshers moved across the township and stopped here three weeks ago to cut, bundle and thresh the last wheat crop we'll be responsible for. The field has been burned of its stubble, cleared and ready for plowing. From experience I know that life will spring up from the blackened earth this fall as the wheat kernels will sprout and flourish. Everything has a cycle on the farm. You plant, tend the fields, harvest the crop and start all over again. Our cycle is over on this land. Another farmer will start over the cycle tomorrow.

Star School, standing forlornly on the corner of our farm, is empty for the summer, except for a few socials. I notice the star emblem on the front of the white building needs painting. Mrs. Robinson named it the Lone Star School, because it was the first school in this area. We homesteaders sacrificed time and what little money we had to hire a teacher and build a school.

Star School

Most of us had little or no schooling in Sweden, but we made sure our children were educated. I remember a traveling teacher that came to our farm for a few weeks when I was little, but it was not enough to really learn much. We girls spent most of our time tending the cows or doing housework, not learning to read. In many ways, I learned along with my children here at Star School.

The grass has grown tall around the white, wooden-framed building, but not the baseball diamond. Every Sunday evening, the week's worth of grass and weeds that tried to grow is trampled down as the neighborhood boys take the Lord's day of rest to meet and work off farm responsibilities. I won't be here to hear their noisy laughter this Sunday evening.

Turning west on the path between our land and Olsons and heading for the creek, I think of our first day on our land. A harsh dose of reality in the form of a thunderstorm and flood that night made us quickly learn to respect nature. This creek was our only source of water when we first moved here. I carried water in buckets from the creek to our camp a quarter mile away, and washed clothes on the banks until we got our well dug.

The creek has flooded the farm several times in the past. Most times, the flood waters just backed up into our bottom fields and corrals and was gone in a few hours time. Today the creek is almost dry as we cross the bottom with our buggy. Looking down under the trees that canopy the bank, I can see a tiny puddle of stagnant water. All kinds of animal prints are imprinted around the water's edge. Possum, birds, even a set of bobcat tracks. They depend on the water like we do.

Fields on the west side of the creek feature long rows of waist-high corn that will be husked by someone else this fall. Peter recently cultivated the young corn for its last time. The lush green stocks seem to grow overnight in this heat. I'll miss not having fresh field corn to can next month.

A little whirlwind of dust whips the corn leaves as it twists through the field. It seems to dissipate as fast as it formed. These fields have seen drought years where dust devils seemed to be the only thing that would generate growth on this land. We toured here when the corn finally gave up and withered away to dry stalks before tasseling. A few years the grasshoppers were so thick, they ate the leaves and just left the veins on the stock. Old farmers have seen all kinds of conditions in their fields. Luckily for us, there have been more good than bad.

Olson's fields on the north are clean of weeds and orderly in their straight rows. Joe and his brother, Gottfrid, are good farmers. Besides corn, they have a field of sorghum cane and alfalfa. The boys and their parents have been good neighbors. We will still be visiting their farm since it is Julia's home now.

We stop at the end of the field and just listen before getting out of the buggy. The gentle tone of the water below the river bank's edge is barely audible today.

We're under the spread of the giant mulberry tree. The area below it is covered with late overripe berries that have fallen from the branches. Last month I came down with Julia and the children to pick enough berries for several pies and pints of jelly. I mainly sat in the shade of the wagon, watched the baby and reminisced how I picked every fruit cluster off this tree when there wasn't much on it yet when it was a young tree. Christina was a little younger than Julia's oldest child, Earland, but they both had about the same amount of juice stains on their clothes by the time we were done picking. I hope Julia keeps the tradition of picking from this very tree with her children and grandchildren. This was some of the very first fruit that we ate off this land.

This river, and the land surrounding it, was our food source our first years before we raised livestock and a garden. Carl hunted and trapped wild animals and I cooked whatever he brought home. It might have been a tough old possum or coon, but at least it was nourishment. We tanned the hides for coats, caps or blankets.

Getting out and looking over the steep bank, we see the muddy water meandering down river at a dawdling pace. It is in no hurry today. A sand bar sits in the middle of the river at this point. Sand has caught around a tree whose roots on the bank gave way. By one grain of sand at a time, it has turned into a sizable bank.

The whole family has spent many enjoyable hours fishing and exploring the water's edge. We've dug for river clams and marveled at their iridescent shells. We followed tiny deer tracks in the spring and were rewarded with the sight of a tiny spotted baby deer. The boys spent hours watching a family of beavers industriously working to chew through trees, drag them down into the river and build their hut. Trees and plants have been dug from the banks and replanted around our farm. The river has enriched and sustained our lives.

I've also known this river at its worst, too. Storms have changed the level and currents in an instant, from a low, calm river to a deep, life-threatening rage. I once stood up on the railroad bridge and watched a wall of water descend at such a neck-breaking pace, that I ran from the track, sure that the water was going to swallow me up from it's banks. Sometimes the roar of the river crashed off hunks of bank as it banged its way downstream during flood times. In the past 50 years we've seen slight bends in the river become ever-widening ones.

The flood of '03 was the worst we've ever seen. Rain storms and tornadoes plagued the area for the months of May and June. Finally, the river banks couldn't hold the water any longer and it spread for miles. Every farm or town within a few miles of the river was flooded. The Isaacsons, up on higher ground, looked down on the river valley and saw water as far as they could see.

The Star School section line was even under water. Passenger and freight trains were stranded in Bridgeport for six days because of flooding in mid-June. Cyclones killed people, destroyed farms and bridges in the area. Hail 11 to 13 inches in diameter punctured roofs and windows.

And it wasn't just our immediate area that was being flooded and damaged. In Salina brick buildings were unstable and caving in because of basements full of water. Barns washed away in the force of the water in Gypsum. Over 1000 drown and tens of thousands of people were left homeless in the Kansas City area. It was a flood we fortunately survived, and will always remember.

We had water in every building on the farm. That's about the only time I can remember flood water getting into our house and well. We kept the milk cows and horses tied up at John Magnuson's place to the east of us on higher ground. Thirty-five pigs drowned in the waters before we could save them.

Heading back south on our west property line, we cross the railroad tracks that divide our land. We have walked this track many

104

Bridge over Smoky Hill River by farm

times when the roads were bad and we couldn't drive to Bridgeport. Whether to get supplies, mail, or catch a train to Lindsborg or Salina, this track has been our lifeline to civilization for over thirty years.

I remember the meeting held at Star School with the railroad officials when they first laid out the plans to build a railroad to connect the western part of the state with the civilized east. Both Bridgeport and Assaria were vying for the opportunity to have their town bisected by the railroad tracks, because it meant people would come to their town for trade. It ended up that Bridgeport won. The track would be built through Gypsum and head to Bridgeport and Lindsborg. Our land was in their right-away, so part of our acres we worked so hard to plow were bought out by the railroad.

Peter's steady hand gives me balance as I stiffly crawl out of the buggy. Reaching behind the seat, I draw out my walking stick. Years ago, this stick and I had the strength to kill the dangerous rattlesnakes that threatened my little children. This tree limb has always been my staff of life. Now I lean on it for this last walk. We've stopped at the middle of the west boundary of our original land. This is the highest point. The land slopes down to the river to the west and down to the creek on the east. From here we can survey all the land we struggled to tame into cultivated fields. And we succeeded.

From this point looking east in 1868, we couldn't even see our sod dugout, since it blended into the native prairie. It was easy to walk right past it if it wasn't broad daylight. Now down below us is a cluster of buildings and corrals. The new barn, shining brightly with its dark red coat contrasts dramatically with the light cream colored two-story house. The pens are empty now, but have held hundreds of cattle and pigs over the years. Trees dot the landscape where there were absolutely none in the beginning.

Looking at the farm from the south

Back in the buggy and cutting across the alfalfa field, we follow the creek as it meanders to the southeast, ending up in our south meadow. In this pasture our animals grazed contently on the grass during summers and sought shelter in the timber along the creek during winter. Come early spring, we often walked the creek in the pasture to check on newborn calves.

Cattle weren't the only thing that enjoyed this meadow. It was always a favorite place for young people to congregate for picnics. The horses that pulled the buggies were released to munch grass with the cattle while the girls spread blankets under the trees on the grassy bank of the creek. Huge picnic baskets, brimming with food and jugs of lemonade, were carried to the spot from the buggies. On several occasions in the fall, there would be bonfires too.

Peter stops the buggy along the creek for one more stop. Walking the bank, he finds a shady spot and spreads an old quilt below the trees for us to sit on. There is a little puddle of water where the creek goes under the road bridge. The only motion on it is a tiny ripple when a dragonfly skims the scum-covered surface of the stagnant water.

The wet burlap sack sewed around the gallon jug has kept the lemonade cold. We pass the jug between us. The tin cups we would normally have with us are packed. Out of my apron pocket, I pull out a cloth napkin revealing two *skorpor* wrapped inside. I baked and packed a huge batch of this hard sweet bread for the trip to America. We had to bring our own food for the voyage and this bread kept up our strength for weeks. Skorpor was packed in our food basket for the trip from Illinois to Kansas too. It seemed fitting to have some today for our last journey.

From our vantage point, we can see the narrow bare path the milk cows have used twice a day to walk from this pasture, along the creek, through the corrals, to the barn. No grass has even had a chance to grow in this path, until now.

As my eyes follow the path, I look up into the walnut tree and spy green nuts starting to form. I've used the walnut meats for baking and the walnut hulls for dyeing fabric a dark brown. I'll have to remind Julia to gather some this fall for me.

Dreading the final quarter mile, we finally ease back in the buggy and head north again, back to the house. The farm seems smaller now, a patchwork of fields, instead of one big span of grass. The little spindly trees we hand planted around each field to keep out the stray longhorns from the cattle drives, have matured into a thicket of living fence line. We follow this row north until we come back to the farm yard.

I've made the circle of our land like I did 51 years ago. When we first saw the land, I wondered if we had made a mistake in leaving Illinois. But I had no choice then but to challenge the land and make it our home. We didn't have the money to move back. Even with all the ups and downs of farming, this land has been good to us. I hope the next young couple that farms this land, tours the farm and appreciates its qualities.

This week I've wondered what life would have been like if we had stayed in Sweden. Chances are, several of our children would have starved a slow death. Here in America they have all prospered. Yes, there have been some bad memories here, like the death of my first husband and the loss of a child that never got the chance to experience life, but that could have also happened if we had stayed in the Old Country.

But you can't change things by wishing back the past. I've learned to enjoy what I have and make the most of it. Even though it is time to leave the farm I've loved for over 50 years, I'll remember the past with fondness and enjoy the present and future in our new home. No matter where we live, family will always be close by. It's the spirit of family that has held us together, no matter if we lived in Sweden, on this farm, or the next place. Our roots have always grown strong, wherever we lived, and has sustained us in bad and good times.

With the help of our family, the three of us will move into town this afternoon. My oldest daughter moved with me to this farm, now the youngest will help me move on to the next home.

I've walked through the entire house, opened every door, staring inside the rooms to burn the vision of the details into my memory. Touching the walls, I've closed my eyes and traced the details of the woodwork and wallpaper. My footsteps echo since the house is now empty. It reminds me of the sound when the house was first built and we hadn't moved the furniture in yet. Hollow, needing love and warmth of a family. Soon another family will live in this house and the sound will change back.

As I turn to shut the attic door, the Swedish picture catches my eye. I had leaned it up against the wall with the glass inward when I cleaned the attic Tuesday. Apparently the brown backing blended it into the unfinished walls and we forgot to carry it downstairs when we cleaned out the room. Walking toward it, I stumble on something. A small stubby pencil is stuck lengthwise in a crack between the floor boards. Prying it out I drop it in my apron pocket.

I've been thinking about leaving some possession behind, as a reminder that I lived here. Picking up the picture, I turn it around and hang it on the nail to the left of the window. Stepping back to look at it, I automatically put my hands down and feel the pencil in my pocket. Taking the picture back down, I write my name on the wall behind that space and sign it,

I lived on this land from 1868 to 1919.
Mary C. Runeberg

As an after thought, I signed my Swedish name underneath.

Maja Kajsa Johandotter Svensson Runeberg

After hanging the picture back in place, I leave the room, shut the bottom door, stick in the peg to hold it shut, swing the top door up and turn the wooden block. Descending the stairs sideways, with my back against the north wall, I keep looking back until I'm at the bottom step.

Noise and dust going by the house heading north means the family caravan has started down the road. Everyone's vehicle has a load as they haul the last boxes and trunks into our new house in town. The children and grandchildren have already walked through the house and said their own good-byes. Peter is waiting outside for me.

I had been debating which door to finally leave the house from. There are four main doors, from different additions to the house. I walked through to decide which door to use. I walk out the back porch door that we used for everyday use. Slowly going around the side of the house, running my hand along the siding, I re-enter the house through our bedroom door, to reminisce where our children were born. After going down the small hallway to the parlor, I open the parlor door where I've greeted guests for years. Gazing out at the glider swing on the porch and beyond, flashes of happy times came to mind. This door was only used for company. I could hardly see the doorknob through my tears as I close this door. The next time I might be in this house, I will be the guest using this door, instead of the greeter.

Straightening my shoulders, I march through the dining room and out its south door. This was the first door I walked into when we built the sandstone section of our house in 1870, and I am leaving the same way.

After walking through the yard gate, I turn and look back once more before climbing into the waiting vehicle to take me away from the home I've known for all these past years. For a split second I am looking back on our home in Sweden, and feeling the same panic of leaving the familiar. But then I remind myself that the future is ahead of me, just as it was then.

After we turn out of the lane, Peter stops in the middle of the road to take one last look at the farm. We sit here for a long time, hating to leave our farm. His feelings were the same as mine as he squeezed my hand. The farm had been good to us and we will always cherish it's memory, but it is time to go.

Peter and Kajsa

Left to right: Peter, Mabel, Julia, Carrie, Alfred, Alma, Willie, Christina and Kajsa- circa 1918

Family Chart

Kajsa and Carl Swenson

Their children:
1. Anna Christina, married Swan I. Nelson in 1889.
   child: Anna
2. Anders Wilhelm, married Minnie Granquist in 1900.
   children: Martha and Viola
3. Alma Eleanor, married Nels Runneberg in 1900.
   children: Arnold, Petunia, Lawrence, Florence,
                   Carl, Emmett, Alice
4. Alfred, married Gertrude Marie Nelson in 1902.
   children: Elvera, Evelyn, Carl, Melvin, Carrol, Chrystella
5. Carolina, married Per Sjogren in 1896.
   children: Myrtle and Verna

Kajsa and Peter Runeberg

Their children:
6. Julia Linnea, married Joseph Olson in 1911.
   children: Earland, Linette, Rozella, Helen
7. Mabel Adelaide, married Axel Linn in 1920.
   no children

DIED

MARY RUNEBERG

Born, June 15, 1844
Died, July 14, 1920
Age 76 years, 29 days

Funeral Service at the home, Sunday, July
18th, at 1:45, and at the Swedish Lutheran
Church in Assaria, Kansas
at 3:00 o'clock

AT REST

WEDNESDAY, JUNE 17, 1925
At 11:30 A. M.

PETER RUNEBERG
Age 71 Years, 5 Months and 5 Days.

Funeral Services will be held from the home Sunday,
June 21 at 2:00 p. m., and from the Immanuel Lutheran
Church, Salina, Kansas, at 2:30 p. m. Interment will be
at Assaria, Kansas.

114

Swedish Glossary

det är dags: it's time
Julotta: early morning Christmas church service
ljuskrona: means lighted crown: a Christmas decoration
                with candles on the end of the branches
lutfisk: dried stockfish, soaked, then cooked
Kvinnornas Missionsförening: Women's Missionary Society
prärieblomman: prairie flower
skorpor: rusks: dried bread with cinnamon and sugar
smörbakelser: butter cookies shaped in a tart pan
spritz: butter cookie
Svensk Psalmbok: Swedish Psalm Book
svärmor: mother-in-law
tack så mycket: thank you very much
var så god: you are welcome

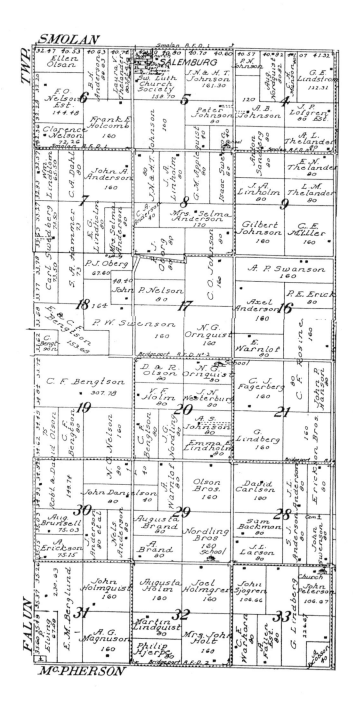

1920- Saline County, Kansas

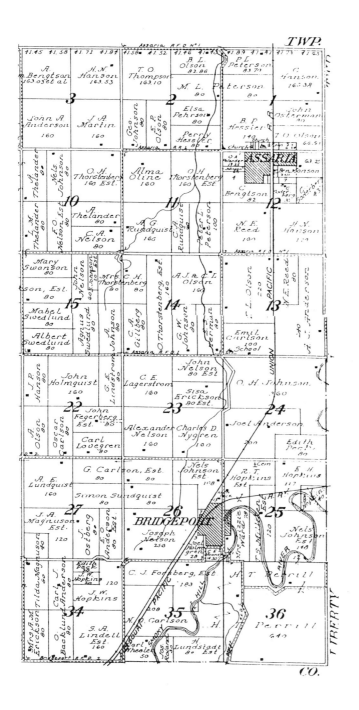

Township 16 South. Range 3 West.

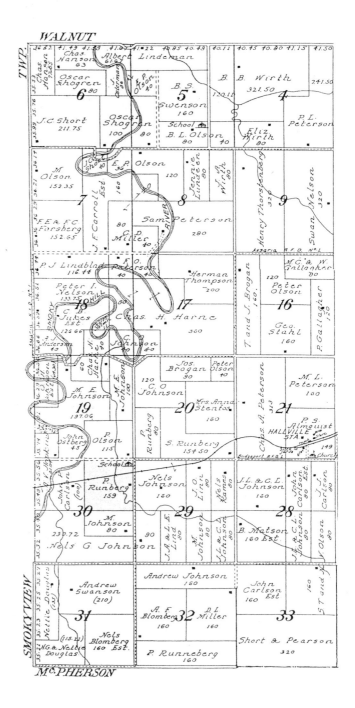

1920- Saline County, Kansas

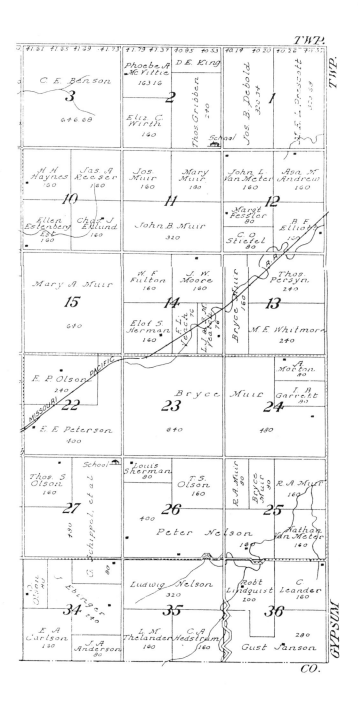

Township 16 South. Range 2 West.

About the Author

A door may close in your life but a window will open instead.

Linda Hubalek knew years ago she wanted to write a book someday about her great-grandmother, Kizzie Pieratt, but it took a major move in her life to point her toward her new career in writing.

Hubalek's chance came unexpectedly when her husband was transferred from his job in the Midwest to the West Coast. She had to sell her wholesale floral business and find a new career.

Homesick for her family and the farmland of the Midwest, she turned to writing about what she missed, and the inspiration was kindled to write about her ancestors and the land they homesteaded.

What resulted was the *Butter in the Well* series, four books based on the Swedish immigrant woman who homesteaded the family farm in Kansas where Hubalek grew up.

In her second series, *Trail of Thread*, Hubalek follows her maternal ancestors, who traveled to Kansas in the 1850s. These three books relive the turbulent times the pioneer women faced before and during the Civil War.

Planting Dreams, her third series, portrays Hubalek's great-great-grandmother, who left Sweden in 1868 to find land in America. These three books trace her family's journey to Kansas and the homesteading of their farm.

Linda Hubalek lives in the Midwest again, close to the roots of her writing career.

The author loves to hear from her readers. You may write to her in care of Butterfield Books, Inc., PO Box 407, Lindsborg, KS 67456-0407.

Bibliography

PUBLISHED MATERIAL

40th Anniversary Album of the Evangelical Lutheran Congregation of Salemsborg, 1869-1959.

100th Anniversary Yearbook, Bethany Lutheran Church, Lindsborg, Kansas. Wichita, Kansas: Jeffery's of Kansas, 1969.

Allender, Etta Wallace. *A History of One-room Public Schools of Saline County, Kansas.*1992.

Assaria, Kansas, 80th Anniversary, 1886-1966.

Axelrod, Alan and Phillips, Charles. *What Every American Should Know About American History: 200 Events that Shaped the Nation.* Holbrook, Mass.: Bob Adams, Inc. Publishers, 1992.

Billdt, Ruth. *Pioneer Swedish-American Culture in Central Kansas.* Lindsborg, Kansas: Lindsborg News-Record, 1965.

Billdt, Ruth, and Jaderborg, Elizabeth. *The Smoky Valley in the After Years.* Lindsborg, Kansas: Lindsborg News-Record, 1969.

Bramwell, Ruby Phillips. *City on the Move: The Story of Salina.* Salina, Kansas: Survey Press, 1969.

Building by Faith, from yesterday . . . for tomorrow. The Assaria Luterhan Church, Assaria, Kansas 1875-1975. Lindsborg, Kansas: Lindsborg News-Record, 1975.

Cox, Charles Philip. *Horses in Harness.* Greendale, Wis.: Reiman Associates, Inc., 1987.

Deaths and Interments—Saline Co., Kansas 1859-1985. Compiled by the Smoky Valley Genealogical Society and Library Inc., 1985.

Johnson, Maurine. *Swedish Footprints on the Kansas Prairie.* Hillsboro, Kansas: Multi Business Press, 1993.

Lessiter, Frank. *Horse Power.* Milwaukee, Wis.: Reiman Publications, Inc., 1977.

Lindsborg Efter Femtio År. Rock Island, Ill.: Augustana Book Concern, 1919.

Lindsborg pa Svensk-Amerikansk Kulturbild från Mellersta Kansas. Rock Island, Ill.: Augustana Book Concern, 1909.

McCutcheon, Marc. *The Writer's Guide to Everyday Life in the 1800s.* Cincinnati, Ohio: Writer's Digest Books, 1993.

Mills, Robert K., Ed. *Implement & Tractor: Reflections on 100 Years of Farm Equipment.* Overland Park, Kansas: Intertec Publishing Co., 1986.

Minnes Album—Svenska Lutherska Församlingen, Salemsborg, Kansas, 1869-1909. Rock Island, Ill.: Augustana Book Concern, 1909.

Seventy-Fifth Anniversary 1875-1950, Assaria Lutheran Church, Assaria, Kansas. Topeka, Kansas: Myers and Co., 1950.

Vid Fyrtioårsfesten, Svenska Evangeliskt Lutherska Assaria Församlingen i Assaria, Kansas, Den 6-8 Okt. 1916.

NEWSPAPERS

The Lindsborg News and Record

The Salina Daily Union

The Salina Sun

The Semi-Weekly Salina Republican Journal

The Weekly Salina RepublicanJournal

Published and unpublished materials listed in the bibliographies of *Butter in the Well* and *Prärieblomman* were also used.

Order Form

Book Kansas!/Butterfield Books
P.O. Box 407
Lindsborg, KS 67456
1-800-790-2665
www.bookkansas.com

SEND TO:

Name _____

Address _____

City _____

State _____ Zip _____

Phone # _____

❏ Check enclosed for entire amount payable to
   Butterfield Books

❏ Visa   ❏ MasterCard   ❏ Discover

Card # [ ][ ][ ][ ] [ ][ ][ ][ ] [ ][ ][ ][ ] [ ][ ][ ][ ]

Exp Date [ ][ ]

Signature (or call to place your order) _____ Date _____

ISBN #	TITLE	QTY	UNIT PRICE	TOTAL
1-886652-00-7	Butter in the Well		9.95	
1-886652-01-5	Prarieblomman		9.95	
1-886652-02-3	Egg Gravy		9.95	
1-886652-03-1	Looking Back		9.95	
	Butter in the Well Series - 4 bks		35.95	
1-886652-05-8	**Cassette: Prarieblomman**		9.95	
	Note cards: Butter in the Well		4.95	
	Note cards: Homestead		4.95	
	Postcards: Homestead		3.95	
1-886652-06-6	Trail of Thread		9.95	
1-886652-07-4	Thimble of Soil		9.95	
1-886652-08-2	Stitch of Courage		9.95	
	Trail of Thread Series - 3 books		26.95	
1-886652-11-2	Planting Dreams		9.95	
1-886652-12-0	Cultivating Hope		9.95	
1-886652-13-9	Harvesting Faith		9.95	
	Planting Dreams Series		26.95	
			Subtotal	
			KS add 6.4% tax	
Shipping & Handling: per address ($3.00 for 1st item. Each add'l. item .50)				
			Total	

Retailers and Libraries: Books are available through Butterfield Books, Baker & Taylor, Bergquist Imports, Booksource, Checker Distributors, Ingram, Skandisk and Western International.

RIF Programs and Schools: Contact Butterfield Books for discount, ordering and author appearances.